The Spectacles:
A Collection of Short Stories

From the "Major Works" series

CJS Hayward

CJS Hayward Publications, Wheaton

**The reader is invited to visit cjshayward.com
and amazon.com/author/cjshayward.**

Table of Contents

Preface

"The Spectacles" invites us to a question: "What would life be like if we could see the true beauty in others?" It is one of over a dozen different short stories here; others cover the Gospel recontextualized, or freedom from shame, or what is beautiful in a life filled with suffering. Here are stories to provoke and challenge, to invite the reader to grow.

You are invited to read as many or as few of these stories as you like.

A Picture of Evil

Once upon a time, there was a king. This king wished that his people know what evil was, so that his people could learn to recognize and flee from it. He issued a summons, that, in a year, all of his artists should come to him with one picture, to show what was evil. The best picture would be displayed to the people.

In a year, they all appeared at the king's palace. There were very few artists in the kingdom, but those who were there were very skillful, and worked as they had never worked before. Each brought a picture beneath a shroud.

The king turned to the first artist who had come. "Jesse, unveil your picture, and tell us its interpretation."

Jesse lifted the cloth. Against a background of blackened skulls was a dark green serpent, the color of venom and poison, with eyes that glowed red. "Your Majesty, it was the Serpent whose treacherous venom deceived man to eat of the forbidden fruit. The eye is the lamp of the body, and the Serpent's eye burns with the fires of Hell. You see that beyond the Serpent are skulls. Evil ensnares unto death and outer darkness."

The court murmured its approval. The picture was striking, and spoke its lesson well. The king, also, approved. "Well done, Jesse. If another picture is chosen, it will not be because you have done poorly. Now, Gallio, please show us your work."

Gallio unveiled his painting. In it was a man, his face red and veins bulging from hate. In his hand, he held a curved dagger. He was slowly advancing towards a woman, cowering in fear. "Your Majesty, man is created in the image of God, and human life is sacred. Thus the way we are to love God is often by loving our neighbor. There are few blasphemies more unholy than murder. You have asked me for a picture to show what evil is, that your subjects may flee from it. This is evil to flee from."

The court again murmured its approval, and the king began to shift slightly. It was not, as some supposed, because of the repellent nature of the pictures, but because he had secretly hoped that there would be only one good picture. Now, it was evident that the decision would not be so simple. "Gallio, you have also done well. And Simon, your picture?"

Simon unveiled his picture, and people later swore that they could smell a stench. There, in the picture, was the most hideous and misshapen beast they had ever seen. Its proportions were distorted, and its colors were ghastly. The left eye was green, and taller than it was wide. The right eye was even larger than the left, red, bloodshot, and flowing with blood; where there should have been a pupil, a claw grotesquely protruded. It was covered with claws, teeth, fur, scales, blood, slime, tentacles, and bits of rotted flesh; several members of the court excused themselves. "However it may be disguised, evil is that which is sick, distorted, and ugly."

There was a long silence. Finally, the king spoke again. "I see that there are three powerful pictures of evil, any one of which is easily a masterpiece and well fit to show to the people. Barak, I know that you have been given artistic genius, and that perhaps your picture will help me with this difficult decision. Unveil your picture."

Barak unveiled his picture, and an awestruck hush fell over the court. There, unveiled, was the most beautiful picture they had ever seen.

The picture was in the great vault of a room in a celestial palace. It was carved of diamond, emerald, ruby, jasper, amethyst, sardonyx, and chrysolite. Through the walls of gem, the stars shone brightly. But all of this was nothing, compared to the creature in the room.

He carried with him power and majesty. He looked something like a man, but bore glory beyond intense. His face shone like the sun blazing in full force, his eyes flashed like lightning, and his hair like radiant flame. He wore a robe that looked as if it had been woven from solid light. In his left hand was a luminous book, written in letters of gold, and in his right hand was a sharp, double edged sword, sheathed in fire and lightning.

The king was stunned. It took him a long time to find words, and then he shouted with all of his might.

"You fool! I ask you for a picture of evil, and you bring me this! It is true that fools rush in where angels fear to tread, and that, like unthinking beasts, they do not hesitate to slander the glorious ones. What do you have to say for yourself and for this picture? I shall have an explanation now, or I shall have your head!"

Barak looked up, a tear trickling down his cheek. "Your Majesty, do you not understand? It is a picture of Satan."

Stephanos

*The crown of Earth is the temple,
and the crown of the temple is Heaven.*

Stephan ran to get away from his pesky sister—if nothing else he could at least outrun her!

Where to go?

One place seemed best, and his legs carried him to the chapel—or, better to say, the temple. The chapel was a building which seemed larger from the inside than the outside, and (though this is less remarkable than it sounds) it is shaped like an octagon on the outside and a cross on the inside.

Stephan slowed down to a walk. This place, so vast and open and full of light on the inside—a mystically hearted architect who read *The Timeless Way of Building* might have said that it breathed—and Stephan did not think of why he felt so much at home, but if he did he would have thought of the congregation worshipping with the skies and the seas, the rocks and the trees, and choir after choir of angels, and perhaps he would have thought of this place not only as a crown to earth but a room of Heaven.

What he was thinking of was the Icon that adorns the Icon stand, and for that matter adorns the whole temple. It had not only the Icons, but the relics of (from left to right)

Saint Gregory of Nyssa, Saint John Chrysostom, and Saint Basil the Great. His mother had told Stephan that they were very old, and Stephan looked at her and said, "Older than email? Now *that* is old!" She closed her eyes, and when she opened them she smiled. "Older than email," she said, "and electric lights, and cars, and a great many of the kinds of things in our house, and our country, and..." her voice trailed off. He said, "Was it as old as King Arthur?" She said, "It is older than even the tale of King Arthur and his Knights of the Round Table."

As he had kissed the relics, he had begun to understand that what made them important was something deeper than their old age. But he could not say what.

But now he opened the doors to the temple, smelled the faint but fragrant smell of incense—*frankincense*—and was surprised to see another Icon on the stand. (Oh, wait, he thought. There were frequently other Icons.) The Icon was Saint Mary of Egypt. (This Icon did not have any relics.) He looked at the Icon, and began to look into it. What was her story? He remembered the part of her story he liked best— when, very far from being a saint at the beginning of her life, she came to a church and couldn't go in. An invisible force barred her, and a saint, the Mother of God, spoke to her through an Icon. Stephan vaguely remembered Father saying something about how it was also important how after years of fasting from everything but bread or vegetables, she was discovered but refused to go back to places that would still have been a temptation to her.

She was very gaunt, and yet that gauntness held fierce power. When he had looked into the Icon—or through it, as one looks through a window—he kissed her hand and looked at the royal doors, light doors with a kind of wooden mesh (it was beautiful) and a tower of three Icons each. The royal doors were at the center of the low, open wall that guarded the holy of holies within the temple, a special place crowned by the altar. The top two Icons told the place, not of the Annunciation **to** the Mother of God, but the

Annunciation **of** the Mother of God. He looked into the pictures and saw the Annunciation **of** the Mother of God: not when the Archangel said, "Hail, O favored One! The Lord is with you," but when the Virgin listened and replied, "Behold the handmaiden of the Lord. Let it be done to me according to your word."

The spine of Eve's sin was snapped.

Death and Hell had already begun to crumble.

After looking through these pictures—it was not enough to say that he simply looked at them, though it was hard to explain why—he turned around and was absorbed into the Icon painted as a mural on the sloped ceiling that was now before him.

If that was the answer to Eve's sin, this was the answer to Adam's sin.

The Icon was an Icon the color of sunrise—or was it sunset? Then he saw something he hadn't seen before, even though this was one of his favorite Icons. It was an Icon of the Crucifixion, and he saw Christ at the center with rocks below—obedience in a garden of desolation had answered disobedience in a garden of delights—and beyond the rocks, the Holy City, and beyond the Holy City a sky with bands and whorls of light the color of sunrise. Now he saw for the first time that where Christ's body met the sky there was a band of purest light around it. Christ had a halo that was white at the center and orange and red at the sides—fitting for the Christ who passed through the earth like a flame.

The flame made him think of the God Who Cannot Be Pushed Around. This God sent his Son, who was also the One Who Cannot Be Pushed Around. In his teaching, in his friendship, in his healing the sick and raising the dead, every step he made was a step closer to this, the Cross. And yet he did this willingly.

Stephan turned, and for a moment was drawn to the mural to the right, which was also breathtakingly beautiful. Two women bore myrrh (the oil that newly chrismated Orthodox have just been anointed with) to perform a last service—the last service they could perform—to a dearly loved friend. And yet they found an empty tomb, and a majestic angel announcing news they would not have dared to hope: the Firstborn of the Dead entered death and death could not hold him. Its power had more than begun to crumble. But then Stephan turned back, almost sharply. Yes, this was glory. This was glory and majesty and beauty. But Stephan was looking for the beginning of triumph...

...and that was right there in the Icon the color of sunrise. The Cross in itself was the victory of the God Who Cannot Be Pushed Around. However much it cost him, he never let go of his plan or his grace. Christ knew he could call for more than twelve legions of angels—but he never did. He walked the path the Father set before him to the very end.

Stephan stood, his whole being transported to the foot of the Cross. However long he spent there he did not know, and I do not know either. He looked through the Icon, and saw—*tasted*—the full victory of the God Who Cannot Be Pushed Around.

When he did look away, it was in the Light of that God. Everything now bore that Light. He went over to the relics of the patron saints of his land, and though they were much newer than the relics of Saint Gregory of Nyssa, Saint John Chrysostom, and Saint Basil the Great, that didn't seem to matter. It was like dust from another world—precious grains of sand from Heaven—and the Icon of Saint Herman of Alaska and Saint Innocent holding up a tiny building was richly colorful—"like a rainbow that has grown up," he heard one of the grown-ups say.

Then he walked over to the Icon of Saint Ignatius of Antioch, holding a scroll that was open partway, with his letter to the Romans: "Let me be given to the wild beasts, for by their means I can attain to God. I am God's wheat, and I am being ground by the teeth of the beasts, so that I may an"—but here the quotation stopped, leaving him wondering. That Icon itself was one of several old-looking, yellowed Icons—though not nearly the oldest around—held in a deep, rich brown wooden frame carved with grapevines and bunches of grapes, as many things in that room were carved (though some had intricate interwoven knots). Stephan said, "I want to be a martyr just like you, Saint Ignatius. Pray for me."

Then he walked over to an Icon that was much smaller, but showed a man standing besides a rustic settlement with an outer wall and turrets and doors and buildings inside. It looked medieval to him, and he wished he could enter that world. It was darkened and yellowed and had a gold leaf sky, and something was written at the top, but he couldn't read it because it was in a very old language: Old Slavonic.

Right by that Icon was Saint Anthony, the father of all monastics. He had a piercing gaze, and Stephan had the feeling he needed to confess something—but he couldn't think of anything besides his bout with his sister, and she had been a pest. He looked away.

Stephan looked at the Icon on the left of the wall, and saw the prince, Saint Vladimir, with buildings and spires behind him that looked like they were having a party.

Then Stephan stood in front of the main Icon of the Mother of God holding God the Son, though he stood some distance back. The background was gold, and this drew him in a different way than the Icon of Saint Vladimir. This more than any other did not work like a photograph. (Or at least he was more aware of this now.) It might look odd to people who were just used to photographs, but you could say that a photograph was just a picture, but to say this was just a picture would show that you missed what kind of a picture you were looking at. But he had trouble thinking of how. He didn't so much sense that he was looking inot the Icon as that the Mother of God and the Son of God were looking at him. He didn't even think of the Icon being the Icon of the Incarnation and First Coming.

Then he looked at the Icon of the Last Judgment, where Christ the King and Lord and Judge returns holding a book of judgment, a book that is closed because there is nothing left to determine.

He thought intensely. The First Coming of Christ was in a stable, in a cave, and a single choir of angels sung his glory. The Second and Glorious Coming he will ride on the clouds, with legion on legion of angels with him. The First Coming was a mystery, one you could choose to disbelieve— as many people did. There will be no mistaking the Second Coming. In the First Coming, a few knees bowed. In the Second Coming, every knee will bow, in Heaven and on earth and under the earth, and every tongue will confess that Jesus Christ is Lord, some in bliss and rapture and others in utter defeat. At the First Coming, a lone star in the sky heralded Christ's birth. At the Second Coming, the stars will fall to earth like overripe figs and the sky recede as a vanishing scroll.

What were those chilling, terrifying words of Christ? "Depart from me, you who are damned, into the eternal fire prepared for the Devil and his angels. For I was hungry and you gave me nothing to eat, thirsty and you gave me nothing to drink, sick and in prison and you did not visit me, lacking clothes and you did not give me the dignity of having clothes to wear." Then the condemned will say, "Where did we see you hungry and not feed you, or thirsty or sick or in prison and not take care of you?" And the King and Lord and Judge will say, "I most solemnly tell you, as much as you did not do it for the least of these brothers and sisters, you did not do it for me."

Stephan looked at the Icon and said, "I wish Dad would let me give money to beggars when I see..." Then his voice trailed off. The words didn't feel right in his mouth. He looked at the solemn love in the Icon, and then his mind was filled with the memory of his sister in tears.

He slowly backed down from the Icon, feeling the gaze of the King and Lord and Judge. He turned to almost run— he was in too holy of a place to run, and...

Something stopped him from leaving. After struggling

inside, he looked around, and his eyes came to rest on the Icon of the Crucifixion that was the color of sunrise. Now he had not noticed them earlier this time, but he saw the Mother of God on one side and the beloved disciple on the earth. What had he just heard in church on Sunday? "Christ said to the beloved disciple, who is not here named because he is the image of every disciple, 'Behold your Mother,' and to his Mother, 'Behold your Son.' Listen to me very carefully. He did not say, 'Behold another man who is also your son,' but something much stranger and more powerful: 'Behold your Son,' because to be Orthodox is to become Christ." Stephan started to think, "Gold for kingship, incense for divinity, myrrh for suffering—these are Christ's gifts but he shares them with the Church, doesn't he?" He looked up, and then looked down.

"But I need to go and apologize for hurting my sister."

Then Christ's icon walked out the door.

The Commentary

Memories flitted through Martin's mind as he drove: tantalizing glimpses he had seen of how people really thought in Bible times. Glimpses that made him thirsty for more. It had seemed hours since he left his house, driving out of the city, across back roads in the forest, until at last he reached the quiet town. The store had printer's blocks in the window, and as he stepped in, an old-fashioned bell rung. There were old tools on the walls, and the room was furnished in beautifully varnished wood.

An old man smiled and said, "Welcome to my bookstore. Are you—" Martin nodded. The man looked at him, turned, and disappeared through a doorway. A moment later he was holding a thick leatherbound volume, which he set on the counter. Martin looked at the binding, almost afraid to touch the heavy tome, and read the letters of gold on its cover:

**COMMENTARY
ON THE OLD AND NEW TESTAMENTS
IN ONE VOLUME
CONTAINING A CAREFUL ANALYSIS OF
ALL CULTURAL ISSUES
NEEDFUL TO UNDERSTAND THE BIBLE
AS DID ITS FIRST READERS**

"You're sure you can afford it, sir? I'd really like to let it go for a lower price, but you must understand that a book like this is costly, and I can't afford to sell it the way I do most other titles."

"Finances will be tight, but I've found knowledge to cost a lot and ignorance to cost more. I have enough money to buy it, if I make it a priority."

"Good. I hope it may profit you. But may I make one request, even if it sounds strange?"

"What is your request?"

"If, for any reason, you no longer want the commentary, or decide to get rid of it, you will let me have the first chance to buy it back."

"Sir? I don't understand. I have been searching for a book like this for years. I don't know how many miles I've driven. I will pay. You're right that this is more money than I could easily spare—and I am webmaster to a major advertising agency. I would have only done so for something I desired a great, great deal."

"Never mind that. If you decide to sell it, will you let me have the first chance?"

"Let's talk about something else. What text does it use?"

"It uses the *Revised Standard Version*. Please answer my question, sir."

"How could anyone prefer darkness to light, obscurity to illumination?"

"I don't know. Please answer my question."

"Yes, I will come to you first. Now will you sell it to me?"

The old man rung up the sale.

As Martin walked out the door, the shopkeeper muttered to himself, "Sold for the seventh time! Why doesn't anybody want to keep it?"

Martin walked through the door of his house, almost exhausted, and yet full of bliss. He sat in his favorite overstuffed armchair, one that had been reupholstered more than once since he sat in it as a boy. He relaxed, the heavy weight of the volume pressing into his lap like a loved one, and then opened the pages. He took a breath, and began reading.

INTRODUCTION

At the present time, most people believe the question of culture in relation to the Bible is a question of understanding the ancient cultures and accounting for their influence so as to be able to better understand Scripture. That is indeed a valuable field, but its benefits may only be reaped after addressing another concern, a concern that is rarely addressed by people eager to understand Ancient Near Eastern culture.

A part of the reader's culture is the implicit belief that he is not encumbered by culture: culture is what people live under long ago and far away. This is not true. As it turns out, the present culture has at least two beliefs which deeply influence and to some extent limit its ability to connect with the Bible. There is what scholars call 'period awareness', which is not content with the realization that we all live in a historical context, but places different times and places in sealed compartments, almost to the point of forgetting that people who live in the year 432, people who live in 1327, and people who live in 1987 are all human. Its partner in crime is the doctrine of progress, which says at heart that we are better, nobler, and wiser people than those who came before us, and our ideas are better, because ideas, like machines, grow rust and need to be replaced. This gives the reader the most extraordinary difficulties in believing that the Holy Spirit spoke through humans to address human problems in the Bible, and the answer speaks as much to us humans as it did to them. Invariably the reader believes that the Holy Spirit influenced a first century man trying to deal with first century problems, and a delicate work of extrication is needed before ancient texts can be adapted to turn-of-the-millenium concerns.

Martin shifted his position slightly, felt thirsty, almost decided to get up and get a glass of water, then decided to continue reading. He turned a few pages in order to get into the real meat of the introduction, and resumed reading:

...is another example of this dark pattern.
In an abstracted sense, what occurs is as follows:

1. Scholars implicitly recognize that some passages in the Bible are less than congenial to whatever axe they're grinding.

2. They make a massive search, and subject all of the offending passages to a meticulous examination, an examination much more meticulous than orthodox scholars ever really need when they're trying to understand something.

3. In parallel, there is an exhaustive search of a passage's historical-cultural context. This search dredges up a certain kind of detail—in less flattering terms, it creates disinformation.

4. No matter what the passage says, no matter who's examining it, this story always has the same ending. It turns out that the passage in fact means something radically different from what it appears to mean, and in fact does not contradict the scholar at all.

This dark pattern has devastating effect on people
from the reader's culture. They tend to believe that
culture has almost any influence it is claimed to; in
that regard, they are very gullible . It is almost
unheard-of for someone to say, "I'm sorry, no; cultures
can make people do a lot of things, but I don't believe a
culture could have *that* influence."

It also creates a dangerous belief which is never
spoken in so many words: "If a passage in the Bible
appears to contradict what we believe today, that is
because we do not adequately understand its cultural
context."

Martin coughed. He closed the commentary slowly,
reverently placed it on the table, and took a walk around the
block to think.

Inside him was turmoil. It was like being at an
illusionist show, where impossible things happened. He
recalled his freshman year of college, when his best friend
Chaplain was a student from Liberia, and come winter,
Chaplain was not only seared by cold, but looked betrayed
as the icy ground became a traitor beneath his feet.
Chaplain learned to keep his balance, but it was slow, and
Martin could read the pain off Chaplain's face. How long
would it take? He recalled the shopkeeper's words about
returning the commentary, and banished them from his
mind.

Martin stepped into his house and decided to have no
more distractions. He wanted to begin reading commentary,
now. He opened the book on the table and sat erect in his
chair:

Genesis

1:1 In the beginning God created the heavens and
the earth.
1:2 The earth was without form and void, and

darkness was upon the face of the deep; and the Spirit of God was moving over the face of the waters.
1:3 And God said, "Let there be light"; and there was light.

The reader is now thinking about evolution. He is wondering whether Genesis 1 is right, and evolution is simply wrong, or whether evolution is right, and Genesis 1 is a myth that may be inspiring enough but does not actually tell how the world was created.

All of this is because of a culture phenomenally influenced by scientism and science. The theory of evolution is an attempt to map out, in terms appropriate to scientific dialogue, just what organisms occurred, when, and what mechanism led there to be new kinds of organisms that did not exist before. Therefore, nearly all Evangelicals assumed, Genesis 1 must be the Christian substitute for evolution. Its purpose must also be to map out what occurred when, to provide the same sort of mechanism. In short, if Genesis 1 is true, then it must be trying to answer the same question as evolution, only answering it differently.

Darwinian evolution is not a true answer to the question, "Why is there life as we know it?" Evolution is on philosophical grounds *not* a true answer to that question, because it is not an answer to that question at all. Even if it is true, evolution is only an answer to the question, "*How* is there life as we know it?" If someone asks, "Why is there this life that we see?" and someone answers, "Evolution," it is like someone saying, "Why is the kitchen light on?" and someone else answering, "Because the switch is in the on position, thereby closing the electrical circuit and allowing current to flow through the bulb, which grows hot and produces light."

Where the reader only sees one question, an
ancient reader saw at least two other questions that
are invisible to the present reader. As well as the
question of "How?" that evolution addresses, there is
the question of "Why?" and "What function does it
serve?" These two questions are very important, and
are not even considered when people are only trying to
work out the antagonism between creationism and
evolutionism.

Martin took a deep breath. Was the text advocating a
six-day creationism? That was hard to tell. He felt
uncomfortable, in a much deeper way than if Bible-
thumpers were preaching to him that evolutionists would
burn in Hell.

He decided to see what it would have to say about a
problem passage. He flipped to Ephesians 5:

> 5:21 Be subject to one another out of reverence
> for Christ.
> 5:22 Wives, be subject to your husbands, as to
> the Lord.
> 5:23 For the husband is the head of the wife as
> Christ is the head of the church, his body, and is
> himself its Savior.
> 5:24 As the church is subject to Christ, so let
> wives also be subject in everything to their
> husbands.
> 5:25 Husbands, love your wives, as Christ loved
> the church and gave himself up for her,
> 5:26 that he might sanctify her, having cleansed
> her by the washing of water with the word,
> 5:27 that he might present the church to himself
> in splendor, without spot or wrinkle or any such
> thing, that she might be holy and without
> blemish.
> 5:28 Even so husbands should love their wives as

their own bodies. He who loves his wife loves himself.

5:29 For no man ever hates his own flesh, but nourishes and cherishes it, as Christ does the church,

5:30 because we are members of his body.

5:31 "For this reason a man shall leave his father and mother and be joined to his wife, and the two shall become one flesh."

5:32 This mystery is a profound one, and I am saying that it refers to Christ and the church;

5:33 however, let each one of you love his wife as himself, and let the wife see that she respects her husband.

The reader is at this point pondering what to do with this problem passage. At the moment, he sees three major options: first, to explain it away so it doesn't actually give husbands authority; second, to chalk it up to misogynist Paul trying to rescind Jesus's progressive liberality; and third, to take this as an example of why the Bible can't really be trusted.

To explain why the reader perceives himself caught in this unfortunate choice, it is necessary to explain a powerful cultural force, one whose effect cannot be ignored: feminism. Feminism has such a powerful effect among the educated in his culture that the question one must ask of the reader is not "Is he a feminist?" but "What kind of feminist is he, and to what degree?"

Feminism flows out of a belief that it's a wonderful privelege to be a man, but it is tragic to be a woman. Like Christianity, feminism recognizes the value of lifelong penitence, even the purification that can come through guilt. It teaches men to repent in guilt of being men, and women to likewise repent of being women. The beatific vision in feminism is a condition of sexlessness, which feminists call 'androgyny'.

Martin stopped. "What kind of moron wrote this? Am I actually supposed to believe it?" Then he continued reading:

> This is why feminism believes that everything which has belonged to men is a privelege which must be shared with women, and everything that has belonged to women is a burden which men must also shoulder. And so naturally, when Paul asserts a husband's authority, the feminist sees nothing but a privelege unfairly hoarded by men.

Martin's skin began to feel clammy.

> The authority asserted here is not a domineering authority that uses power to serve oneself. Nowhere in the Bible does Paul tell husbands how to dominate their wives. Instead he follows Jesus's model of authority, one in which leadership is a form of servanthood. Paul doesn't just assume this; he explicitly tells the reader, "Husbands, love your wives, as Christ loved the church and gave himself up for her." The sigil of male headship and authority is not a crown of gold, but a crown of thorns.

Martin was beginning to wish that the commentary had said, "The Bible is misogynistic, and that's good!" He was beginning to feel a nagging doubt that what he called problem passages were in fact perfectly good passages that didn't look attractive if you had a problem interpretation. What was that remark in a theological debate that had gotten so much under his skin? He almost wanted not to remember it, and then—"Most of the time, when people say they simply cannot understand a particular passage of Scripture, *they understand the passage perfectly well.* What they don't understand is how to explain it away so it doesn't contradict them."

He paced back and forth, and after a time began to think, "The sword can't always cut against me, can it? I know some gay rights activists who believe that the Bible's prohibition of homosexual acts is nothing but taboo. Maybe the commentary on Romans will give me something else to answer them with." He opened the book again:

> 1:26 For this reason God gave them up to dishonorable passions. Their women exchanged natural relations for unnatural,
> 1:27 and the men likewise gave up natural relations with women and were consumed with passion for one another, men committing shameless acts with men and receiving in their own persons the due penalty for their error.

The concept of 'taboo' in the reader's culture needs some explanation. When a person says, "That's taboo," what's being said is that there is an unthinking, irrational prejudice against it: one must not go against the prejudice because then people will be upset, but in some sense to call a restriction a taboo is de facto to show it unreasonable.

The term comes from Polynesia and other South Pacific islands, where it is used when people recognize there is a line which it is wiser not to cross. Thomas Aquinas said, "The peasant who does not murder because the law of God is deep in his bones is greater than the theologian who can derive, 'Thou shalt not kill' from first principles."

A taboo is a restriction so deep that most people cannot offer a ready explanation. A few can; apologists and moral philosophers make a point of being able to explain the rules. For most people, though, they know what is right and what is wrong, and it is so deeply a part of them that they cannot, like an apologist, start reasoning with first principles and say an hour and a half later, "and this is why homosexual acts are wrong."

What goes with the term 'taboo' is an assumption that if you can't articulate your reasons on the drop of a hat, that must mean that you don't have any good reasons, and are acting only from benighted prejudice. Paradoxically, the term 'taboo' is itself a taboo: there is a taboo against holding other taboos, and this one is less praiseworthy than other taboos...

Martin walked away and sat in another chair, a high wooden stool. What was it that he had been thinking about before going to buy the commentary? A usability study had been done on his website, and he needed to think about the results. Designing advertising material was different from other areas of the web; the focus was not just on a smooth user experience but also something that would grab attention, even from a hostile audience. Those two goals were inherently contradictory, like mixing oil and water. His mind began to wander; he thought about the drive to buy the commentary, and began to daydream about a beautiful woman clad only in—

What did the commentary have to say about lust? Jesus said it was equivalent to adultery; the commentary probably went further and made it unforgiveable. He tried to think about work, but an almost morbid curiosity filled him. Finally, he looked up the Sermon on the Mount, and opened to Matthew:

> 5:27 "You have heard that it was said, `You shall not commit adultery.'
> 5:28 But I say to you that every one who looks at a woman lustfully has already committed adultery with her in his heart.

There is a principle here that was once assumed

and now requires some explanation. Jesus condemned
lust because it was doing in the heart what was sinful
to do in the hands. There is a principle that is
forgotten in centuries of people saying, "I can do
whatever I want as long as it doesn't harm you," or to
speak more precisely, "I can do whatever I want as
long as I don't see how it harms you." Suddenly purity
was no longer a matter of the heart and hands, but a
matter of the hands alone. Where captains in a fleet of
ships once tried both to avoid collisions and to keep
shipshape inside, now captains believe that it's OK to
ignore mechanical problems inside as long as you try
not to hit other ships—and if you steer the wheel as
hard as you can and your ship still collides with
another, you're not to blame. Heinrich Heine wrote:

> Should ever that taming talisman break—the
> Cross—then will come roaring back the wild
> madness of the ancient warriors, with all their
> insane, Berserker rage, of whom our Nordic
> poets speak and sing. That talisman is now
> already crumbling, and the day is not far off
> when it shall break apart entirely. On that day,
> the old stone gods will rise from their long
> forgotten wreckage and rub from their eyes the
> dust of a thousand years' sleep. At long last
> leaping to life, Thor with his giant hammer will
> crush the gothic cathedrals. And laugh not at my
> forebodings, the advice of a dreamer who warns
> you away from the . . . *Naturphilosophen*. No,
> laugh not at the visionary who knows that in the
> realm of phenomena comes soon the revolution
> that has already taken place in the realm of
> spirit. For thought goes before deed as lightning
> before thunder. There will be played in Germany
> a play compared to which the French Revolution
> was but an innocent idyll.

Heinrich Heine was a German-Jewish poet who lived a century before Thor's hammer would crush six million of his kinsmen.

The ancient world knew that thought goes before deed as lightning before thunder. They knew that purity is an affair of the heart as well as the hands. Now there is grudging acknowledgment that lust is wrong, a crumbling acceptance that has little place in the culture's impoverished view, but this acknowledgment is like a tree whose soil is taken away. For one example of what goes with that tree, I would like to look at advertising.

Porn uses enticing pictures of women to arouse sexual lust, and can set a chain of events in motion that leads to rape. Advertising uses enticing pictures of chattels to arouse covetous lust, and exists for the sole reason of setting a chain of events in motion that lead people to waste resources by buying things they don't need. The fruit is less bitter, but the vine is the same. Both operate by arousing impure desires that do not lead to a righteous fulfillment. Both porn and advertising are powerfully unreal, and bite those that embrace them. A man that uses porn will have a warped view of women and be slowly separated from healthy relations. Advertising manipulates people to seek a fulfillment in things that things can never provide: buying one more product can never satisfy that deep craving, any more than looking at one more picture can. Bruce Marshall said, "...the young man who rings at the door of a brothel is unconsciously looking for God." Advertisers know that none of their products give a profound good, nothing like what people search for deep down inside, and so they falsely present products as things that are transcendent, and bring family togetherness or racial harmony.

It has been asked, "Was the Sabbath made for man, or was man made for the Sabbath?" Now the question should be asked, "Was economic wealth made for man, or was man made for economic wealth?" The resounding answer of advertising is, "Man was made for economic wealth." Every ad that is sent out bears the unspoken message, "You, the customer, exist for me, the corporation."

Martin sat in his chair, completely stunned.
After a long time, he padded off to bed, slept fitfully, and was interrupted by nightmares.

The scenic view only made the drive bleaker. Martin stole guiltily into the shop, and laid the book on the counter. The shopkeeper looked at him, and he at the shopkeeper.
"Didn't you ask who could prefer darkness to light, obscurity to illumination?"
Martin's face was filled with anguish. "How can I live without my darkness?"

The Grinch Who Stole Christmas

My dear Wormwood;

I still do not have your report on the status of the yearly festivals. As you have not informed me of the circumstances for several years, I may unfortunately be forced to demonstrate drastic consequences in the case that you fail again to even tell what is happening.

Your affectionate uncle,
Screwtape

Dear uncle Screwtape;

It is about as well as could be expected. This is a time of festivities which we have very little difficulty turning the people away from; it is, also, one of the ones where there is joy and exuberance such that it is very difficult to introduce even a dead and ritualistic approach to ceremony. We have succeeded at least in enticing a handful of people to drunkenness and adultery on one hand, and on the others have slowly been building an interest in sorcery. I am currently contemplating the introduction of a number of grimoires to heighten the interest in spellcraft; unfortunately, this is the rare exception rather than the rule, and we can make very little progress with the great many. I suppose that we should expect greater success at other times of year.

Your nephew,
Wormwood.

My dead Wormwood;

    YOU IDIOT!
    You speak of getting a handful of people interested in spellcraft as a great achievement. Were you here, you would see that your letter caused me to engage in something not unlike men's prestidigitation; I immediately raised my arm and extended my middle finger.
    So, you have enticed a tiny handful. Whoop-de-doo. Nobody minds that you've chopped down a tree or two, but we are here to burn a forest.
    It is evident that your abysmal lack of understanding of temptation has produced the silliest possible results. If you are going to tempt a man, TEMPT him. A large shipment of spellbooks to devout people is not productive. Have you no idea why you are trained to masquerade as an angel of light?
    Use the right tool for the right job.
    I want a full analysis of the situation, and a preview of any ideas, just to ensure that you do not do anything dumber.

Your affectionate uncle,
Screwtape

Dear uncle Screwtape;

It is the season when they celebrate the greatest gift they have ever received; namely, when the Enemy became one of them and died to create a way of escape from our trap of sin.

There are two basic intertwined ways in which they celebrate, and we have been able to do very little to stop either.

The first is by thanksgiving and enjoying what they have been given. They come to friends and family; they pray, sing songs, eat, drink, and be merry. A few we've managed to get drunk on the wassail or abstain from it as if it were an evil thing, but that is a chink here and there; we have had trouble making it larger. There is a wholehearted attitude of thanksgiving and worship at all the gifts which they've received; the time when we've set famine to take away some of their food only seems to make them all the more grateful and all the more prayerful.

The second is by giving each other gifts. Whether the gifts are simple or costly, they are heartfelt; they celebrate the gift given them by giving gifts to each other. Even in the lands where an evil duke has imposed harsh taxes on the peasant, so that they have little to give, their little gifts are taken as seriously as more lavish gifts from people who do have enough to live on.

I have been trying to deter them from the celebration and the gift giving, but results have been frustrating to the extreme.

Your nephew,
Wormwood

My dear Wormwood;

Having taken some time to think, I should like to temper some of my previous remarks. Nor that your bungling incompetence does not warrant them, but I should like you to be better informed.

There is both an individual and a corporate side to sin. The individual side is of extreme importance. Our father below personally tempted Job, and it is not an understatement to say that every last person should be tempted as far as possible. By chipping at one tree at a time, it is possible to clear cut a forest. (The importance of the individual is so great that it may be an interesting temptation to make people appear to be nothing but individuals). When the temptations facing a society do not affect a person, it is perfectly acceptable to give some variation. Once in a while, even that can be worked into a good plan for even greater corporate sin. It is spectacular to have a few become prostitutes and a great many become Pharisees; a few become witches, and a great many become witch hunters.

As important as individual sin is, it is now your responsibility to see to corporate sin, and tempt the society as a whole.

There is something I should like to remind you about the nature of sin.

Man is created to embrace what is good. Even in his fallen state, even with the power that we hold over them, that man still somehow desires to embrace the good is so true that it dictates the nature of temptation. When we tempt, it is necessary to give a candy coating to that sin with what is good. Sexual sin is only possible when we twist the tremendous goodness of human sexuality; idolatry can not exist except as an exploitation of the need of man to worship the Enemy.

There is a time and a place to use intimidation, terror, and force, but your attempts here to either tempt solid believers with sorcery, or make their celebrations impossible by physical hardship, are clumsy and inappropriate. Gold which is passed through fire only grows purer; that is why you see their devotion flowering. Instead, why don't you appear as an angel of light and lull them to sleep?

There is a note about patience... Though occasionally we manage the sudden and sharp, it is much better in most cases (including this one) to work ever so slowly. So slowly that there doesn't seem to be any real progress; so slowly that everything appears to them to be as they want it. If you suddenly hold a candle by a frog, it will jump away. If, instead, the frog is placed in a pot of cool water and the candle beneath the pot, it will never notice; nothing constrains it from jumping out, and yet you need only wait for the ever so slowly growing heat to destroy it. Be patient; wait for decades or centuries if need be.

Now stop wasting your energy on stupid spellbooks, droughts, and taxes. Take away these hardships; for now, I want you to only make things easier. Help their economic systems be productive; don't take away from the laughter at the feasts. If you find an opportunity to get someone drunk at a festival, then by all means take it, but don't worry about having things now. Just do as I have said, and wait.

Your affectionate uncle,
Screwtape

Dear uncle Screwtape;

It is ten years now, and I have done as you have said. I do not understand why; they enjoy the festivities as much as ever, giving and receiving gifts in a manner that enjoys each other; enjoying each other in a manner that loves and worships the Enemy. By all counts, things have only gotten worse. Am I to continue to wait?

Your nephew,
Wormwood

My dear Wormwood;

Patience, my dear. Patience. If you continue, you are making more progress than you think. Now, I still don't want you to do anything spectacular. Only give an idea to an inventor here, an economist there. Don't introduce anything nasty; just make the economic system more productive, and do nothing to impede their thoughts of giving generous gifts at this season.

Your affectionate uncle,
Screwtape

Dear uncle Screwtape;

It is twenty years since I last wrote you, and I still do not see the point. People have more money; they are giving it generously. The hungry are fed; the naked are clothed. The season is one of great festivity, and, as ever, they give generous gifts. Am I to continue?

Your nephew,
Wormwood

My dear Wormwood;

Still, you need patience. Now, I want you to do two things:

First of all, continue to increase the productivity of their economic system.

Second of all, without actively disparaging love for God or their neighbors, I want you to use the season to cause them to think about how good their material possessions are, and look forward to it.

Give it ten more years, and write back.

Your affectionate uncle,
Screwtape

Dear uncle Screwtape;

I have succeeded in making them think about the goodness of their material possessions (which I still do not fully understand; most of the time, you have had me delude people into thinking that the material is evil and an obstruction to spiritual growth; I am now emphasizing that truth in the matter as you say, and I don't see any real progress). It is ten years; what should I do now?

Your nephew,

Wormwood

My dear Wormwood;

   Now, slowly, slightly, introduce seeds of greed. Not too much; just a little. And give them more money.
   It is the time to twist, and everything you twist should be done, at least at first, in a slow and slight, imperceptible manner. Twist the good of the celebration and the presents just a little; that's all that it takes, for the moment. Just make the goodness of God and the gift the season celebrates seem less of an easy thing to think about than the goodness of all the material gifts.
   Give it ten years or so, and write me back again.

Your affectionate uncle,
Screwtape

Dear uncle Screwtape;

   Wow. Though it's been slow, this work has been beginning to show some real results. Though every gift given by one person is a gift received by another, people are thinking of this much less as a time to give gifts, and much more as a time to receive them. I've now made it a major part of their economy; people are beginning to look forward very much to all of the Christmas gifts they can receive.
   Should I continue as I have been?

Your nephew,
Wormwood

My dear Wormwood;

There is something to be said about greed. Like most other sins, it produces satiety for the moment, but over time it yields only insatiety. Those who have enough and are content with what they have remain content; those who have much with greed grow more wealthy and less satisfied. More than that, many of those who have the most material possessions enjoy them the least; time to acquire possessions, and worry for them, becomes a consuming desire. A powerful chief executive officer who can buy anything he wants, will enjoy much less the leather seats of his Porsche, the view from his yacht, the beauty of his art collection, than many children of more modest means enjoy a chain of dandelions and a grape flavored lollipop.

Just continue, and put some serious thought into the trash that you teach them to prize. I could give more detail, but I think you're beginning to understand. Write me back in a few more years; tell me what happens.

Your affectionate uncle,
Screwtape

Dear uncle Screwtape;

Things have really been taking off.

The holiday celebration has become a tremendous commercial extravaganza, the best time of year when people look forward to getting glowing plastic dolls and combination pizza oven/clothes dryers. I have gone wild with the items which are produced. I've made one device so that much of the time people spend "together" is distant and mechanical, with no eye contact and no touch. They now have, and look forward to ever more advanced entertainment devices with blinking lights and spectacular sound effects, bright and shiny enough to distract people the emptiness within, and ever becoming more effective. (You might also be pleased to learn of the content; although the type of devices would facilitate excellent strategy games, I've made graphic violence seem more and more attractive; a wonderful entertainment. Now I don't even have to be slow and patient in making a more realistic sadism; all that needs to be done is put somewhere in the storyline that you're the hero and morally justified in wading through blood. (I'm working on taking that away as well)) I'm making sure that the games are solitary by nature; you can't really play these games with your friends the way you can play cards, having a friendly chat as well as thinking about what to do as the next move. On a scale of glitz and convenience, they seem far more attractive than reading a book, holding a friend's hand, going for a walk, or having a relaxed meal together. I've been working on a faster, exciting, frantic pace for the entertainment, and people are "learning" that having fun means moving at a breakneck speed; leisure is beginning to be considered boring. There is a great air of celebration and festivity, and an air of gifts; the facade is tremendous.

I think that the festival is mostly under control. Should we make a shift in strategy?

Your nephew,
Wormwood

My dear Wormwood;

Congratulations! You have passed this portion of your training with flying colors. Although I have more experience in this matter and have enjoyed many times sitting back and watching the flames as a society crumbles under the weight of its own sin, you have celebrated trivia to an extent that even I find astounding. My hat is off to you.

For now, your responsibilities (which you have made much easier) have been shifted; as you have so masterfully learned your lessons in corporate sin, it is now time for you to learn the next lesson. Your next area of training will be in the area of heresy, a battleground to which we are shifting focus.

I look forward to seeing what will come of your apprenticeship there.

Your affectionate uncle,
Screwtape

A Glimpse Through a Crystal

I lay on my bed, half-awake, half-asleep, the spectres of dreams beginning to flit through my mind. I saw a castle, a bog, a car with computer screens for its wheels, and many other fleeting images before my mind, when the forms and images began to coalesce.

I saw myself a little boy, blonde-haired, blue-eyed, filthy, and clothed in tattered rags. I was at the end of a pathway, at a pair of massive iron doors, set in a wall of granite that reached as far and as high as the eye could see. On these doors were bronze knockers. I reached, and struck the door; it resounded, as of thunder. I struck the door a second time; it resounded again, and I could sense something — a presence? I know not how to name it. Then my hand reached and knocked the door a third time, and the sound echoed, grew louder, stronger. I stood in place only because I was too terrified to run, and then a blast of light seared the air and shattered the doors. A god came out — he looked majestic enough to be a god, although I could not see his face, for it was covered with a veil — and reached his hand down to me, and said, "Welcome, traveler. I am come to show you the world that is to come. I am to show you Heaven."

I stared in awe and fear, a thousand questions on my mind. And he stood, with a repose that drove away fear. This time, something of the little boy was not only as I saw myself appear on the outside, but inside me; I somehow lost my guile and dignity, and said, "You know what every theologian dreamed of. Can you give me theology from Heaven?"

He laughed, a laugh that burned me and yet was somehow good. He said, "I am sorry, Jonathan. I cannot give you that, because there is no theology in Heaven. It isn't needed. It is one of the brightest lamps that is no more because the Lamb of God himself is our light. When the perfect comes, the imperfect will pass away. Did you want an answer to some area that Christians debate?"

I thought, and answered truthfully, "No. I — I don't know how to explain it. I want something bigger than that."

The god looked at me, and said, "You have answered well. Calvin, Beza, and Arminius are all up here, all in accordance with each other, and none of them has changed his mind. At least not over the points that Calvinists and Arminians debate. There were plenty of other points where they were wrong. Theology is work well worth doing; it contributes to God's glory, but the best of theologians make quite a few errors. Keep seeking the heart of God, the something bigger, and you will find it. What else do you want to know?"

"Do you have laughter still, I hope?"

"Yes, certainly."

"Could you tell me a few jokes from Heaven?"

"No. I will not mock you with things that are too heavy for you. Your funniest jokes have the barest seed the full-grown plant that lives in Heaven and nourishes everyone; you would be destroyed by our humor."

I looked around, and saw a faint emanation of light from beyond the doorway, a vanishing light; mist and darkness were beginning to appear, and the image looked vague and hazy. I asked, "Why can't I see?"

The being before me said, "You don't see. Or, rather, I am seeing with you and for you. Your eyes cannot bear the load of even my veiled face. I appear to you as you are asleep, beginning to dream, but no such thing exists with us. Sleep is an image of death, and has no place in Heaven. Yet only when you are sleeping is your guard down low enough to let Heaven in."

I asked, "Why should I be granted the special privilege of seeing Heaven?"

He said to me, "It is not nearly so rare a privilege as you think. Heaven is breathed by much of art, literature, music, by friendships, deeds, prayer; in many of these things, the people have insights of Heaven, only not consciously. A great many works you ignore breathe Heaven in a way you will never come close to. The Father is dealing with you as he chooses to deal with you, just as he is dealing with others as he chooses to deal with them. Are you ready to come in?"

I hesitated and said, "One more question. Theology won't exist in Heaven; laughter will exist aplenty, too real for me to bear its form. I have some guesses about mathematics, which I will not venture to guess. Will I see anything that I know in Heaven?"

He said, "Yes, indeed, a great many things. You will come to see things in Heaven that will make you wonder how you ever saw them on earth without seeing Heaven in them. The custom among believers of holding hands when praying — community and touch (yes, I know you've written a treatise on touch) naturally accompanying communion with God — exists here, filled with the resurrection life as never before. The blessed here who join hands in prayer are totally present to God and totally present to each other — save that it is not only soul-body touching soul-body, but resurrected spirit-body touching resurrected spirit-body. It is a form of communion with God and man. At least that is as much of it as I can tell you in the words of your language. You who wield your language with skill and power have struggled with its limitations, while still a mortal who has never touched the lifegiving energy of the Great River — nor shall you see it tonight. You may see Heaven when you are with me, as you may see Brazil by riding about Rio de Janeiro for an hour on a bus — that is to say, you cannot see one part in a thousand of what is there, nor can you comprehend one part in a thousand of what you see. You will still learn much. Jonathan, you are really not that far off from joining us; your life on earth is passing, fleeting, however many times it may appear to drag; when you will die, you will look around you and say, 'Am I in God's presence already? That was short.' Then you will drink in full from the wellspring of truth —

"Jonathan, I know why you thought but did not ask about mathematics. Mathematics exists here, as an art form — you were right when you thought of all mortal mathematics having to pass through the gates of finiteness. It has to be decidable in a finite time. That is no longer part of man; we can look and immediately know the answer to any of your great unsolved questions. As to how there can still be mathematics when every person can immediately see the answer to the hardest question — I can't explain it to you, but I assure you that God provides an answer to that more stunning than anything a mathematician on earth will ever know. Eye has not seen, ear has not heard, nor has any mind imagined what God has done with the things his children treasure.

"Come, take my hand. We will pass through the doorway together."

I gasped as he took my hand. It was as if I was holding a burning coal. I looked at my hand, and saw to my surprise that I was looking at the hands of a man again, one whom the fire did not wound. Then the god gave me a pull, and I passed through the blazing portal.

It was with a disappointment that I looked around and saw that I was only in a candy store.

I looked at the wall of glass bowls skeptically, not being in a particular mood for candy. My host said, "Come on!

Take as much as you want! It's on me." I took a colorful assortment of candies, and then went out into a sunny field. We stood, looked at the clouds for a while, and then dove into a pool of water. After swimming, he asked me, "Do you want to come to an amusement park? There are roller coasters there unlike any you've seen on earth."

I hesitated, and said, "This isn't much like what I expected in Heaven. This is like what one of my professors called a Utopia of spoiled children. I expect to see pleasure in Heaven, but if Heaven only offers early pleasure — is this all there is to Heaven?"

My host looked at me and said, "You are quite the philosopher. Pleasure is not all there is to Heaven, but God told me to bring you in by this gateway. You need to become as a little child to enter the Kingdom of Heaven, and there is something a little boy sees when he is told, 'In Heaven you can eat all the candy you want,' that you do not. Become as a little child. Would you like some cotton candy?"

I tried to submit to God's will; I'm not sure I got my attitude right, but I tried at least to do the right thing. So I took the candy, and — have I been blind all these years? I know it sounds presumptuous, but I think I really did taste that candy as a little boy would. It left me thirsty, and I am sure it is only because I was in Heaven that it did not leave a big sticky mess all over my face and clothes, but I *tasted* it — sheer, simple bliss. I've heard the old quotation about how a child can't believe that making love is better than ice cream; at that point, perhaps only partly because I am not married, I began to suspect that that statement stems from a forgetfulness of what a child experiences when he eats ice cream — something that is the highlight of a day, the highlight of a week, something that can make a bad day into a good day.

Some people came along, and we began talking, and it wasn't until a good bit into the conversation when I realized that the conversation was switching fluidly between languages — Italian one moment, Arabic the next, then

Sanskrit, then the unbroken language from before the Curse of Babel, the language of the Dawn of Creation — and I began to cry. One of the things I know I can never have in this life is a mastery of all languages — and something in Heaven, perhaps even that cheap candy, had affected me so that I was able to move among languages and cultures among the gods and the goddesses that surrounded me. There was something else I don't know how to describe — a change that was beginning to be wrought in me. It wasn't so much that I was enjoying what was around me, as that I had an enjoyment coming through who I was. And it was not a cause of pride.

Then, as it were, a veil was torn, and I saw one — what can I call it? a rock, or a flame, or a pulsing mound of energy, unmoved and yet dancing, and around it a constellation of little rocks, each one both like the first rock and totally unlike any other. They were all part of a dance, a dance which combined total order with total freedom — and I was part of the dance! I was aware of a kind of communion with the other dancers; space did not separate us. I would not have been more honored if they had all been spinning about me; there is something about it that I cannot describe, even badly.

The dance continued, and as it continued I saw myself walking through a vast hallway, with floors of marble and shimmering golden trees. There was a stand, and on it lay open a massive book. My host opened it, and I only glanced at the pages — enough to see that it recorded the entire story of creation, from Eden to the Second Coming. My life was written on it, every pure thought and action, every sin; I sat stunned that such a thing could be.

"Every place in Heaven is special, unique," my guest said, "and this is a place of remembrance, of story. The special, sweet, fleeting time on earth that each of us had, is remembered for the goods it had that will not exist here. Choosing the right when one's nature is warped and sinful, making disciples of unbelievers, penitence, forgiveness, and ten thousand other things, from marriage to even theology — they do not exist for us, except as a far off memory. We stand clothed in the good deeds of our life on earth — what we could do in the limited time we had. You have a very special place, part of the tiny minority of runners who approach the finish line, while the rest stood outside, cheering. This is the Story of how we came to be, and it is your Story too. Cherish your time as mortal man; it will not last long. You have not long before the perfect comes and the imperfect disappears. You know how children always wish to grow up, how they rush on, and how adults see childhood as a special time. You want to be through with the race, to have received your crown. Rightly so. At the same time, wish to make the best use of the fleeting moments, of the scarce time before you enter into glory. Before you will know it, many of the goods you know now will be only a memory.

"I would like to show you one more thing. Walk this way." He took me, and opened a door, to a place that seemed to open out onto a countryside, or a palace. The palace had a courtyard, a pool in which to swim, a view onto forest. Inside were books, and meeting places, and a tinkering room, and a gallery of artwork. "You know that our Lord said, 'In my Father's house there are many rooms.' This is one of those rooms. It is a room that the Father has prepared for a believer, knowing all of his life and his virtues and his good works. Each one holds things in common with others, and is different. And they're connected, though you can't see the connections now. Would you like to know whose room you are looking at?"

"Yes, very much. I would like to meet him," I said.

"It's your room, Jonathan. And you haven't seen the tenth part of it. You will forever be king over a corner of Heaven, having this place in which to commune with God and invite other people over — and visit their rooms. It is impossible on earth to be friends with a great many people — but not here."

As I was listening to my guide, I heard footsteps behind me. I looked, and saw a Lamb next to me, soft and gentle. I took it into my arms, and it nestled against my heart. I held the Lamb for a while, and then said, "This guardian fills me with the terror of his majesty; how is it that you do not?" The Lamb looked into my eyes and said, "All this in time you shall understand — when you do not need to. I will hold you in my heart then, as I hold you in my heart now. Would you like to come here? For real?"

I thought and said, "It would not be the best thing. I have longed many times for Heaven, but then where would my creations be? I hope that the time will pass quickly, but I have work to do on earth. Lord, please help me bear the time until then, and let it be fruitful! But I want to enter into Heaven after living to the full the lifetime of work you have for me — whether it is a long lifetime or being killed in a car accident on the road to work tomorrow. I want to come to Heaven through earth."

He said, "You have chosen well, mystic. It will not be that long. And I will always be with you."

I awoke with a jerk, and looked around. 9:58 PM. Time to get a good night's sleep and be rested for tomorrow. And pray for God's providence in my work.

The Metacultural Gospel

I want to tell you about my best friend, Nathaniel. When we were getting to know each other, Nathaniel told me that he was God come down in human form. I thought for a moment and said, "If that's true, you aren't doing a very good job of it." He laughed, and said, "You're probably right."

Where can I begin to describe him? Perhaps you've had this experience. When there's someone you don't know very well, it's easy to say "Yeah, I know him. He's that hockey player who tells the worst puns." But when it's someone you're close to, best-buddies intimate with, then words fail you. I could begin by saying, "Nathaniel was a construction worker," which would leave most people with two impressions. The first impression is that he was strong and had calloused hands, which is true. The second impression is that he wasn't much in the brains department, which is out-and-out false. He didn't have too much in the way of formal schooling — stopped after getting his high school diploma — but Nathaniel was absolutely *brilliant*. I still remember the time when I had him over at my place, reached on my shelf, pulled out the *Oxford Companion to Philosophy*, and read aloud the entry for 'aestheticism', and then began a devastating critique. I don't remember his whole argument, but the first part pointed out that there was an assumed and unjustified opposition between aesthetic and other (i.e. instrumental) attitudes, with an argument that seemed to challenge aestheticism by pointing out that there are other ways of viewing art. He asked if one would challenge the activity of working by pointing out the legitimacy of eating and sleeping. Nathaniel was the first kindred spirit I found in philosophy and other things; he challenged and stretched me, but he was the first person I met who had also thought things I thought no one else would ever understand.

I'd like to explain a little more about the conversation where I told him that if he was God come down in human form, he wasn't doing a very good job of it. How can I put this? It wasn't that he was inhuman — certainly not the sort of thing usually conjured by the term 'inhuman', with some sort of indecency or cruelty or monstrosity. He *was* human — he just challenged my conceptions of what it meant to be human. (I thought *I* was unusual!) Being with him was like realizing one had woken up in a different world — in so many little ways. He fit in, but he wasn't like anybody else.

One of my first shocks came when I saw him chatting, naturally and freely, with some support staff at my office. At first I thought that they were for some reason old friends of his, but he disabused me of that notion. When we talked about it afterwards, I realized the extent to which I had treated support staff like part of the furniture. He seemed to be able to talk with *everyone* — young (he's one of few adults I've known who could enter a child's world and really play), old, rich, poor, American, international, it didn't matter. He could enter the house of a Klu Klux Klansman for dinner and then leave and spend the rest of the evening with a follower of Minister Farrakahn — being on friendly terms with both. He was very good at entering other people's worlds — but he had very much his own world. And there were a thousand little things about it — like how, in his letters, he always wrote 'I' as 'i' and 'you' as 'You'.

I was talking with him about Harold Bloom's treatment

of cultures as caves (as per Plato's "Allegory of the Television, er, Cave"), when I came to the strangest realization. Nathaniel did and did not live in a culture. He did live in American culture in the sense that he spoke the language, literally and figuratively, enjoyed hamburgers, and couldn't handle chopsticks to save his life. You might say that he spoke the culture as would a foreign anthropologist who had given it a lot of study, but I wouldn't. He *owned* American culture. But at the same time, he didn't pick up any of its blind spots. I had given some thoughts to something I call metaculture — something that happens when a kid grows up exposed to multiple cultures, or when someone is really smart and just doesn't think like anyone else does, and doesn't breathe his host culture the way most people do. I had been aware of something metacultural in myself, where I felt like I was a composite of cultures and eras, with something that wasn't captured in any single one of them. I was groping towards something from below, when he had it, all of it, from above. Where I started to climb up to the mouth of the cave, he descended from the world above and met me. I had thought about the phrase "the wave of the past" as an inversion of "the wave of the future", challenging the worship and even concept of modern progress, where each age gets better than the one before; I had been aware of something of real merit grasped by ages past that have been lost in our mad pursuits. And then Nathaniel showed me the wave of Heaven.

Nathaniel spent most of his life as a construction worker. He did a better job at seeming ordinary than I do at least; only his mother Camilla seemed to be able to even guess at who he really was. His family was visiting someone at Wheaton College, and — before I go further, there's something I need to explain about Wheaton.

Wheaton College is a devout place, a religious Harvard if you will. And their approach to religion has its quirks. The temperance movement, which condemned God's creation of alcohol as evil, made a practice of having people sign a Pledge to abstain from alcohol. Wheaton College is one of few places where that practice is alive, and required of every member. Of course they say that they are not making a moral condemnation, but only a prudential measure, but their actions, even what they call their prohibition (which forbids most dancing as well), are deafening.

At the reception, they ran out of soda, and ran out of punch. Camilla kept tugging on Nathaniel's sleeve and asking him to do something. Finally he told them to fill a cooler with tap water — then drew off a cup of the beverage and sent it to the administrator in charge.

It was champagne.

The champagne was dumped, the cooler rinsed out, and filled with water, and it somehow held champagne again. I was embarrassed enough to be drinking champagne (the best I ever tasted) out of a plastic cup. But the administration had a more serious embarrassment to deal with — but I am getting off topic. I was impressed with their response — they are better than their Pledge — and Nathaniel was still welcome on their campus after that happened.

There are other cases where response to his eccentricities did not receive such a positive response. There was one time when we were visiting a really big church, and (after some really impressive instrumental music) the lights were dimmed, and an overhead projector began to display all sorts of computer graphics, and then there was a gunshot, and another, and another; the overhead image disappeared. The gunshots continued; someone turned on the lights, and there was Nathaniel, holding a powerful handgun, shooting the projector. (It was such a strange thing to see a pacifist holding a gun.) I think he emptied a total of about three clips into it, before putting the gun into his pocket. The people around him were cringing in fear, but not terror, or perhaps you could say terror, but not fear; they were afraid, but not of the gun. I think some of them were a little afraid of whatever would make a man angry enough to fire a gun in a church.

About that time, the pastor got over being stunned and glared at him and asked, "How dare you fire a gun in my sanctuary?" He glared back and said, "How dare you take God's sanctuary and making it into a circus? This is supposed to be a house of prayer and worship for all people, and you are making it into mere amusement, a consumer commodity. Is this church set up because these people do not have televisions, that they can flip on and be titillated? Church is a place to disciple men and conform them to God, not a place to conform religion so that it will appeal to spoiled brats. The reason that you are losing people to MTV is that you are doing a second rate job of being an MTV, not a first rate job of being a church. Cleanse this place of your vaudeville filth and make it a place where men are drawn into God's presence to glorify him and enjoy him forever. If not, much worse awaits you than bullet holes in your projector."

There was another time, when we were out of town for Easter and he came to the city's First Baptist. Everybody was wearing business suits and really nice dresses — everybody but Nathaniel. Nathaniel was comfortably arrayed in bluejeans, a plain white T-shirt, and big, heavy, black steel-toed workboots.

There was an invisible stir, and about five minutes into the sermon the pastor stopped, and said, "Young man, I suppose you'd like to explain why the best you can give God on the holiest day of the year is clothing that teenagers wear to McDonald's."

Nathaniel, with perfect composure, said, "Yes, indeed. God is Spirit, and those who worship him must worship him in Spirit and in truth, not in this set of clothing or that set of clothing, nor in this or that outer form of worship or ceremonial observance, nor some particular style of music. You don't know who you are worshipping, if you think (because you can worship God by wearing nice clothes) that nice clothes are necessary for worship. The hour is coming, is indeed already here, when God seeks worshippers who will worship him beyond the external shells that their particular traditions have associated with worship. God is calling. Are you ready to answer?"

It was not long after that that we were out in a van, going to this camp. Duncan was driving; Duncan is a devout man, and a proud graduate of Jehu's Driving School. He was blasting down the highway, which was virtually empty, and everyone but Nathaniel was involved in a very intense discussion; Nathaniel (don't ask me how he does this) was in the back seat, with his head up against a pillow, sleeping. By then I noticed that a wind was rocking our car, and I realized why we were all alone on the road. There was a terrific thunderstorm going on all around, and as I looked out the window there was a flash of lightning, and several of us saw this big twister coming right at the van. I was barely collected enough to jump to the back of the van and shake Nathaniel awake, and asked, "Don't you care if we die?!?" Nathaniel seemed irritated at having been woken up, and asked, "What's the matter? Don't you have any faith?" Then he turned to the storm — or the twister, at any rate, and said, "Peace!" And then, all of a sudden, *everything* stopped. The wind died down, the tornado dissipated, and within minutes we could see the sun shining. It was at that point that I wet my pants.

You have to understand, we were *more* scared after the storm stopped than before. Before then, we had a purely natural fear, the fear that we could quite possibly die. That was fear enough — I don't mean to downplay it — but afterwards we had a purely supernatural fear, the fear that stemmed from watching a ?man? issue commands to inanimate nature and be immediately obeyed. Vulgar and base fears are about what harm can be done. There is a deeper fear that is a kind of awe, the kind of fear we sometimes experience in diminished form when we enter the presence of someone we respect. And at that point we were absolutely terrified. I don't think we would have been any less scared had he already told us that he was God the Son, clothed in flesh just like you or me; at that point, it was as if a veil was lifted, and we got a tiny glimpse into the glory, the splendor, the light that were hidden in this friend who we ate with, who we talked with, and who could pin any two of us in wrestling. Tiny glimpse as it was, it seared our eyes; in retrospect, I'm surprised nobody fainted.

After Nathaniel let us have a couple of minutes to watch the storm dissipate and let us become properly terrified, he did one of the strangest things you could think of. He rebuked us for our lack of faith. At the time, I just sat there, stunned (so did everyone else), but afterwards, I began to have a glimpse into who he was, into his world, into the world that he invited me and invites you.

I am a metacultural, which means in part that I am able to think of my culture, and shift my own position in relation to it and other cultures. One of the things I had been thinking about is the strength of scientism in Western culture as it is now and has been for some time (not all of its history — not by a long shot). Many cultures have been cultures in which people can see ghosts, even if they're not there — they are open to the supernatural; it is real to them. American culture is a culture in which people can't see ghosts, even if they're really there — we are closed to the supernatural; it isn't real to us. Contemporary American culture is the result of monumental efforts to shut out the tiniest glimmer of anything supernatural; this affects not only how people think, but on a more fundamental level what they are and are not able to do. And metacultural awareness, and conscious rejection, of the effects of scientism does not translate into an immediate freedom in one's emotions to believe in miracles.

The sobriety of a recovering alcoholic — hard-earned, the result of swimming upstream — is qualitatively different from the sobriety of someone who has never had a problem with alcohol. For the latter person, sobriety is something that flows easily, something that is almost automatic; for the former, it is something that is difficult, possible only as the result of vigilance. Something of the quality of this difference exists between many cultures of days gone by (and other parts of the world) and our own culture, with regards to belief in the supernatural. There have been places that have breathed the supernatural in ways that are not naturally open to us — and Nathaniel was at least a step beyond that. Sometimes I wondered — still do — at the task before us — as if we were recovering alcoholics, and he brought a bottle of 151, gave us each a shot glass, and said, "You are all going to drink some amount of this beverage and then stop, and not slip into drunkenness." That's something you do with people who don't have a problem with alcohol. It's not something you do with alcoholics. But then, it was just like Nathaniel to believe that we could do things we never would have been able to do by ourselves. And I trust him enough to believe that there was method in what seemed either madness or else the most profound naïveté: "C'mon. I as God incarnate can easily stop a tornado. Why could you possibly be afraid?" Over time, I have even been able to catch glimpses of the method to this divine madness. Beauty is forged in the eye of the beholder; when someone like that trusts you, he makes you worthy of his trust, even if you are not worthy of such trust to begin with.

Anyways, we got to the camp without (further) event, and went into a room; Nathaniel jumped up into the top bunk of the bed in the corner, and curled up so that he was sitting Indian style with his back in the corner, moving his fingers about as if he were playing a keyboard. (This is one of many facets of his private world that people who met him in public might never guess at, but he let his guard down around people who knew him. I'm not even going to try to document all his eccentricities; suffice it to say that this sort of thing was as natural with him as sitting on a chair.)

After changing my pants, I asked him, "What are you

working on?"

He thought for a second, and said, "I'm trying to make a free translation of Bach's Little Fugue in G Minor into English. I think there's more of a connection between the muses than we think, enough so to make translation possible in some cases, if not nearly as easy or universal as translation between natural languages. Have you ever had a basic insight that could have found expression in different forms? I am not exactly trying to translate the finished product of Bach's fugue, as to express in language what Bach chose to express in music."

I asked, "What do you have so far?"

He played the theme and said, "Not much. I'm still trying to figure out whether to translate it as poetry or logic." He paused, and said, "What's on your mind?"

I said, "I was just thinking about church last Sunday. Most of the time I can ignore bad music, but this time the music was bad enough to be a distraction to worship. Why is it that most of the time-honored tunes we use to worship God were never intended to be sung sober, and most contemporary music does not reach even that standard? I don't want to impose a burden on people of 'You must appreciate highbrow music to worship here,' but it seems that there is already a burden of 'You must endure terrible music to worship here.' I know that good music does not make worship, but it seems to me that bad music can break worship. If that music were translated into words, the result would be poorly written and poorly thought out."

Nathaniel looked at me and said, "Sean, the brokenness of this world makes things goofy. I am setting something in motion that will rock the world. Until my work is consummated, until I have returned in glory, there will always be problems. You can see these things perhaps a little more readily than most people; you suffer from them too. You are right to be grieved; the same things grieve me. But you can still live in a world where worship is diminished, where there are laws punishing beggars for begging. The just have always walked by faith with a pure heart, regardless of how much vice is in the world around them. And they have never left my Father's care."

It was after that that we had a really good talk, and I viewed my metaculture differently after that point. I had seen it as a separation between myself and most of mankind; I started to see it as a way of being human, and a part of the catholic plan of salvation, even a part of the tools God was choosing to limit himself to in bringing salvation to the world. And I was able to understand how and why Nathaniel respected the monocultural majority as easily as he did.

In the morning, after a night's dream-thought about metaculture, monoculture, and catholicity, I punched his bunk and said, "Hey, Nathaniel! How many metaculturals does it take to screw in a light bulb?"

He said, "I don't know, Sean. How many?"

I said, "It takes fifteen:

- One to evaluate the meaning of the custom of replacing burnt out light bulbs and think of possible alternatives,

- one to drive off to a store to buy a fluorescent replacement to an incandescent heat bulb, judging the higher price worth the lessened environmental degradation and longer time to replace the bulb with one like it,

- one to read McLuhan and light a small votive candle, preferring the meaning of a candle to that of a light bulb,

- one to go outside under God's light and God's ceiling to see as men have seen for the other two million, four hundred ninety-nine thousand, and nine hundred years of human existence,

- one child to pull up a ladder, unscrew the bulb, and then dissect it to see how it works and whether he can get it working again,

- one tinkerer to assemble a portable light center with ten 120-watt bulbs, wired in parallel, powered by an uninterruptable power supply and a backup generator,

- five Society-for-Creative-Anachronism style re-enactor-ish metaculturals to try to use the occasion to grasp problem solving as understood by the monocultural mindset — one of them holding the bulb, and the other four turning the ladder,

- one critic to point out that, of the last two segments, one wastes an excessive amount of money that could be put to better use, and the other is elitist and demeaning, monoculturalism being a legitimate and God-given form of human existence that has merits metaculturals cannot share in,

- one to observe the variety of facets of the process of changing a bulb into a list, to become an immortal e-mail forward among metaculturals,

- one to say, 'This joke is taking *way* too long and is *far* too complex,' and change the light bulb, and

- one to stick her tongue out at him and say, 'Spoilsport!'"

Without missing a beat, Nathaniel asked, "How many monoculturals does it take to screw in a light bulb?"

I thought for several minutes, trying to think of a good answer, and said, "I give up. How many?"

"One. You're making things far too complex and missing what's in front of your nose."

The problem with people like Nathaniel is that they're just too smart.

We went to breakfast in the dining hall, and after breakfast Nathaniel went up to speak. He cleared his throat and said, "Good morning. Do we have any feminists here? Good. In what I have to say, I'm going to draw heavily on a concept feminism has articulated, namely that rape happens and it should be worked against.

"The human psyche exists in such a way that rape is a devastating psychological wound. It's not just like the sting of a scorpion, where you have a terrible pain for part of a day and then life goes on as it was before; it is a crushing blow after which things are not the same. Perhaps with counseling there can be healing, but it's not something that gets all better just because time passes. Rape is worse than any physical pain; it is a different and fundamentally deeper, more traumatic kind of pain, a pain of a different order.

"I don't know of anyone, feminist or not, who believes in rape because he wants to, because he hopes to live in a world where such things exist. Everyone I've talked with would much rather believe that there is nothing so dark. But it does exist, and disbelief won't make it go away. That is why feminists are going to heroic efforts to promote awareness of rape, to tell people to be careful so that at least some rapes can be prevented.

"I am here tonight to warn you about a place, which I will call Rape because I know of no more potent image to name it. In fact, it is worse than rape, beyond even how rape is worse than a sting. I have given up much, more than you can imagine, to come here, and I will endure much, more than you can imagine, to finish my work, for one reason: to save you all from Rape. If you believed as I believe, you would crawl across America on broken glass to save people.

"You were created spotless, without flaw, and then you wounded yourselves and began to die. It is a fatal wound, one that causes your bodies to lose their animation after seventy years or so, and one that has far worse effects than the destruction of your bodies. Your consciousness will not end when you die; it will rot in a fashion that is beyond death, beyond rape, and it will rot forever. You are all headed for Rape, every one of you, unless you believe in me.

"There is much more I have to tell you, much more that I would like to tell you, grander things about a place of light and love. But that comes only after passing through this doorway. There is a place called Rape, and it is real, and it is more wretched than any vision of torment you can imagine, and I have come to save you from it. Follow me if you want to live."

There was a fairly long and stunned silence after that point; all of the feminists were enraged that a man would take the concept of rape which belonged to feminism and trivialize it like that. All but one. Cassandra neither regarded the concept of rape as belonging to feminism in the sense of an exclusively owned property that others dare not tread on, nor regarded Nathaniel's speech as trivializing rape. At all. This earned censure from the other feminists. She began to follow Nathaniel after that point; she didn't quite believe his conclusions yet, but she had real insight into what would prompt a man to dare to say something like that.

As I reflect back, I can see how someone like Cassandra could live a very lonely life.

That night, Cassandra asked Nathaniel, "What is your favorite movie?"

Nathaniel thought for a second and said, "I don't really have a favorite movie, but I was just thinking for a second about a movie idea that nobody has produced."

Cassandra asked, "What's that?"

Nathaniel said, "Opening scene, there is a prisoner

shackled inside a dungeon cell, with armed guards posted around. Then it shows the hero and his assistants, armed with M-16 assault rifles and one silenced sniper rifle. They sneak up to the complex, the sniper neutralizing three watchmen along the way. One of the men knocks over a glass bottle, and chaos breaks loose when someone hears them and sounds the alarm. There is a big firefight, villainous henchmen dropping like flies. The hero releases the prisoner, and radios for a helicopter to come and pick them up.

"As the last of the hero's friends jump on board the helicopter, one last henchman comes running out, firing a shotgun at the helicopter. The hero takes a .45 caliber handgun, and blasts away his knee.

"The rest of the movie slows down from the action-adventure pace so far, and follows the henchman. For the remaining hour and a half, the movie explores exactly what that one gunshot means to him for the remaining forty years of his life."

Cassandra stood silent for a moment. I could see in her eyes that she was seeing the movie. Nobody said anything for a while; then Nathaniel said, "I want to talk with you more. I need some time by myself now, and then we can really talk."

Nathaniel would depart from us, heading off where nobody could find him, to pray and be with God. This time it was over a month before he returned, and when he did, he looked like a skeleton with skin on — but he had this glow. He was very quiet, and it was a few days before he talked with us about what had happened.

He walked into the wilderness, until he came to a place under some evergreens, by a lake, and by a large stone. He slept on the stone at night, sitting and standing and wandering around in the forest during the day, and praying all the while. He had a sense that something was going to happen — something big, something that would take all of his strengths.

At the end of that time, he was starving, and (on a fifty degree day) hypothermic. He sat there, hungry, shivering, when the Slanderer appeared before him and said, "If you are God and not just a man, strengthen your body so that it will never be touched by hunger or cold, and then you will be freed from physical distractions to pursue your ministry."

Nathaniel said, "I have come as a real man, with real flesh that feels real pain. My ministry is not furthered by selling it out. I would rather die as a real man than have a long ministry by having an inconsistent make-believe body that only affects me so far as is convenient."

The Slanderer said, "You know, that movie idea of yours was something deep. How would you like to be able to make as many movies as you want, to have whatever influence over television and radio, newspapers, magazines, books and internet you care to have? How would you like — no strings attached — to have as much media influence as you want?"

Nathaniel said, "If my mission could have been accomplished by blasting pictures on the sky, I would have done that. That isn't the type of influence I want. I want a real, personal influence where I teach people face to face and touch them. I want to give my friends hugs and kisses. I want something your media can never give."

The Slanderer said, "My, you are picky about my gifts. Here's a suggestion that should interest you. You are coming to offer a salvation, but a salvation that people can only have if they choose it — else they will suffer a torment beyond rape. Why not make everybody accept your gift?"

Nathaniel glared at the Slanderer and said, "Never! I have come to call brothers and sisters, not make computers. My world can be broken as it is only because my Father and I would rather see it broken than break our creatures' free will. The metaphor of Rape is inaccurate in this, that it describes coercion from outside. The Place of Torment is self-chosen, and its doors are bolted and barred from the inside. Rape stands as the final testament to human free will, that my Father would rather see his creatures in everlasting torment than force them into Paradise. Get away from me!"

When Nathaniel said this, the Slanderer left him and angels attended him.

The next few days on the road were interesting. Several of the students at the camp went and followed us. We were on the road to a campustown, and I was beginning to perceive something different about him, something different in his awareness. He was putting weight back on, and there was something new in his eyes.

We arrived at a college campus; we were walking across the quad, and a young woman came up to us and said, "Help me! I am terribly sick, and neither the doctors nor Wicca have been able to make me better. I don't know how much longer —"

There are times when you want to be someplace else, anywhere but where you are now. This was one of those times. The woman became very pale, and lost consciousness; Nathaniel caught her and lay her down on the ground. Then her body became stiff, and from her still, unmoving lips came an ugly, raspy, man's voice, cursing and blaspheming God. Nathaniel alone was not afraid, but his face bore infinite gravity. He looked, and said, "What is your name?"

The demon said, "Our name in English is Existential Angst. Our name in our own language is —"

"Stop!" Nathaniel said. "I know that name, and I know that language, and you are not to utter either of them here."

"Our name is Existential Angst," the demon continued, "and she is ours, all ours, and so is this age."

"She is not yours any more, nor is this age. I have come to set the captives free. Come out of her!"

The voice said nothing more, but there was an unholy presence so powerful it could be felt, and a stench like the stench of rotten eggs, and then they left.

The woman opened her eyes, slowly, as if awakening for the first time, and then looked at Nathaniel. She didn't say anything, just looked, her eyes searching, filled with wonder. Finally, when she had seen what she was looking for, she said, "Thank you." Nathaniel didn't reply. He didn't need to.

By this time, a crowd had gathered, and Nathaniel told Duncan to get a blanket from the van and buy her some bread and some Sprite. Then he looked around — the crowd was very quiet, with everybody looking at him — and Nathaniel stood up, and said, "You can plainly see that I have given something to this woman. What is no less true is that I have something to give each one of you, and you need it.

"Techies sometimes talk about a group of people they call 12:00 flashers. They call them 12:00 flashers, because their houses are filled with appliances with a flashing 12:00. What they mean by the term '12:00 flasher' is something deeper than just 'someone whose appliance clocks happen not to be set'.

"What they mean by '12:00 flasher' is someone who wants the benefits of technology, but is not willing to try to understand how technology works or how to use it. Their appliances flash 12:00 because they will not in a million years spend five minutes experimenting with the buttons or read the manual to see how to set a clock. This mindset affects every bit of technology they own, and invariably something will break — quite possibly because it was misused — and then they will invariably wait until the last minute, when there is an emergency, and ask a techie to "just tell me how to fix it." The 12:00 flasher is involved in a desparate attempt to cut a steak with a screwdriver, and when a techie begins to try to explain why he needs to set down the screwdriver and get a knife, the 12:00 flasher tensely replies, 'I don't have time to put down this screwdriver and go get a knife! I just need you to tell me how to cut this steak!'

"Friends, I am here to tell you that the 12:00 flasher phenomenon doesn't just exist in technology. It exists in human relationships. And it exists in spirituality.

"It's possible to get by as a 12:00 flasher. Nobody died because his living room was perpetually dark because he wouldn't sit down and figure out how to unscrew the top of his lamp and replace the bulb. And, when technological disasters become unlivable, it's usually possible to grab a techie, to the rescue. Never mind what it does to their blood pressure, techies usually can reduce an unlivable disaster to a tolerable disaster. But that isn't how we were meant to live, especially not in relationship with God.

"What is a spiritual 12:00 flasher like? Well, they take many forms, but one thing they all have in common is that, consciously or unconsciously, the question they ask of religion is 'What is the least I can do and still get by?' That question is the wrong question. It's like asking what the least a person can eat and still not starve. Never mind the fact that the experiment is quite dangerous; God did not make or want us to live just barely eating enough not to starve. He made us for rich, abundant live, far from starvation.

"Don't be a 12:00 flasher. Don't ask, 'What is the least I can do and still get by?' Don't run to God in times of crisis, and then when the crisis is over, forget him and go back to life without him. If you have a crisis, by all means, run to God for help. He welcomes that, and sometimes he uses crises to draw people to him as never before. But don't wait for a crisis to seek him out. Seek him out, prepare your spirit, work at a state of right relations with other people, while the going is easy. Don't wait until you're on a sinking boat to learn how to swim. Learn how to swim when you have free time and a swimming instructor.

"I was at the deathbed of an old man, a quiet member of the community who knew everybody by name, who always had time to listen to little children's tales and who would tell his own stories to anybody who wanted to hear. When he was on his deathbed, someone asked him if he would like to hear some Bible verses. He smiled, and to everyone's surprise, said, 'No.' Someone asked him, 'Why not?' He smiled again and said, 'I thatched my hut when the weather was warm.'

"Dear friends, thatch your hut when the weather is warm. You might not be able when there is storm or cold. What is there to do? I wish to mention two things; they are a lifetime's learning, and have been for me. Those two things are love and prayer.

"God loves you, and you are to love him with your whole being. You are to love *every*body. Even your enemies? Especially your enemies.

"Physicists are in search of a grand unified theory, where all of the laws covering all physical phenomena boil down to a few equations that can be written on one side of a sheet of paper. In spirituality, religion, and morality, love *is* that grand unified theory. There are great teachings — of Creation, of repentance, of worship, of Heaven, of grace, of moral law — and for each of them, if you cut into them, cut below the surface, the lifeblood that they bleed, the hidden lifeblood that keeps them alive, is love.

"One of the most important expressions of love, one of the most important incubators for love to grow in, is prayer. The Slanderer laughs at our plans, and scoffs at our power, but trembles at our prayers. Wrap yourselves in a cloak of prayer; pray for other people even as you look at them in passing; pray continually. Prayer is a place where God transforms us, and where God and we working together transform the world. It is a time to step out of time and into eternity, and it refreshes and renews us. Pray incessantly, until you have callouses on your knees from unanswered prayers. You cannot change the world, at least not for the better, on your own power. Prayer is how God makes you into his children and prepares you for results, and then (on his own time — not yours) makes a lasting mark.

"Follow me, each of you, and I will draw you into love

and prayer, into wisdom and truth, into live everlasting."

The people were impressed with his teaching. He spoke as if he knew the truth, not as if he were just sharing his own perspective, his own personal opinion.

It was perhaps because of this that, when we sat down at dinner, a young man approached him and said, "You spoke unlike anyone else I've heard. Do you claim to know absolute truth?"

Nathaniel said, "Yes."

The man said, "But we cannot know absolute truth, only relative perspectives. The quest for absolute truth has failed; all of the major thinkers of our era have renounced it. Who do you think you are to know absolute truth, God? Don't try the old 'You cannot make absolute statements against absolute truth' card; we have perspectives we expect to be binding without being absolute."

Nathaniel said, "As it turns out, I *am* God, but that is rather beside the point at the moment. You say that we cannot know absolute truth. I respond with a dilemma: are you making that claim as absolutely true, or as your own personal opinion? If you are making that claim as absolute truth, then it is self-contradictory, and therefore false, and therefore something I do not need to subscribe to; if you are making that claim as a mere statement of personal opinion, like your preference in ice cream flavors, it is therefore something I do not need to subscribe to. Before you respond, let me add nuance to this dilemma. I know that you would not say that your claim is absolutely true or a personal attribute, but somewhere in between. This dilemma gives you the freedom to choose a position somewhere between the two poles of absolute truth and personal opinion. Most dilemmas have a forced choice, one or the other. Not this one. On this dilemma, you may fall at a mixture of the two horns, that is, you are making a statement that is held to be 80% absolutely true, and 20% your own personal perspective. In which case, it is 80% incoherent, and 20% a personal attribute I can safely

ignore. Or is it 30% absolutely true, and 70% your own
personal perspective? Then it is only 30% incoherent, but it
is 70% a personal attribute I can safely ignore. This
dilemma offers you infinite flexibility in choosing how it
affects you; the end result, however, is that your perspective
is 100% a perspective I am free to ignore."

The young man had nothing to say to this.

There were a number of people who were beginning to
follow him at that point, and I began to see a strand running
through his teaching. Perhaps the best way to begin with it
is by voicing the intuitions it runs counter to.

An obvious reading of what he says is that mankind has
earned everlasting torment in Rape, and he comes through
and offers a way of escape — believing in him, and accepting
a sacrifice that I didn't understand at the time — and it is
worth any amount of earthly effort and sacrifice to save one
soul from Rape. So there are these people who have the
good fortune to know about the escape, and they should
devote their lives to making a difference, to saving as many
people as they can.

That is true, and it is deeply true, and there is an
opposite insight that is a deeper truth, one that is
everlasting.

That insight says that the Father is omnipotent and is
drawing people to himself, drawing people to share in the
glory that God had before the worlds began, not only in a
Paradise after death but here and now, in this world. In
following Nathaniel, the escape from Rape is almost
incidental in importance to communion with God, and our
time on earth is as (Nathaniel was very emphatic about this)
apprentice gods, whose time on earth is a time of
preparation for the time when we will reign in Paradise.

The primacy of the second, mystical interpretation over
the first, pragmatic interpretation is something Nathaniel
was very emphatic about, and that has changed my whole
way of viewing things. I didn't understand it fully until a
moment came when I slapped my head: "How could I not

have seen this before?" I had been listening to the stories of a number of incredibly devout and incredibly dedicated people who were operating in the first mode, who were trying to make the biggest difference, and fell flat on their faces hitting futile barrier after futile barrier. It made no sense. Then I heard stories of people — Wesley, for one — who were like this, and fell on their knees and cried, feeling like utter failures, and in a beggarly, ragged, ragamuffin way, became mystics, sought communion with God. And God gave them that mysticism. Then, sometimes, if he chose, on his time, in his ways, he took some of them and gave them power within the context of that mysticism, and those people shook the world with a force unlike anything they could have ever imagined.

What I came to realize through this is that God wants communion with us, and he wants it so badly that he would rather see a devout, dedicated son working in utter futility, with no results for his toils and watching souls perish, than let some of his children act as mere tools without being drawn first and foremost into communion with him. Drawing people into his presence, not just in the future but here and now, is *that* important to him. God does not want tools. All the angels in a thousand galaxies are his, and if he needed help, he would not tell us. He wants sons and daughters, and he will have us be that and nothing less. My head still spins a little when I think of this.

This account is written so that you may know Nathaniel and the abundant life that he brings, that you may be drawn into communion with God, not just in the world to come but in this world. Therefore I ask you, when you reach the end of this paragraph, to close your eyes, thank God for ten things you're thankful for, and spend five minutes contemplating God's glory. Do it now.

Did you do it? If you did, wasn't that wonderful? Wasn't that the best part of the text? Didn't you want to linger? If you didn't — you're not going to get to Paradise if you won't let Paradise interrupt your reading of a text. This text exists to draw you into communion with God, and if you put the flow of reading ahead of that communion, you still have something to learn.

I've been thinking about how to explain what I want to say next, particularly to most Americans... perhaps the best way is to say that, to the American mind, 'nice' and 'good' mean almost exactly the same thing, and this is a perspective which Nathaniel did not share. Nor do I. 'Nice' is what is left of 'good' after 'good' has been flattened by a steamroller.

Nathaniel was, at times, very nice. He was someone who would look you in the eye and ask, "How are you?" — slowly, because he wanted to hear the answer. He wouldn't just do this with close friends — he was just as ready with strangers whom he could see needed it. But there was something about him that most definitely would not be cut down to fit into being nice. He met with members of the religious community, but his interactions could rarely be described as diplomatic. He lambasted Evangelicals and Catholics on equal terms. He didn't attack mainline Protestants, though. Never. Most of the time, when I mentioned them, he just shook his head and wept.

I'm not going to give a full list of the groups that Saint Nasty offended, primarily because my hard drive only has about nine gigabytes of free space. I do wish, however, to give an illustrative list. There are many more.

- *The gay community.* After a thousand voices had droned on about how AIDS patients are the outcast lepers of our society, Nathaniel said, "The status of AIDS patients in our society is not that of pariahs, but that of sacred cows." He challenged head-on the status of people who die from sexually transmitted diseases as martyrs, and furthermore laid bare how the movement lumps together acceptance and care of homosexuals, acceptance of them as humans, with a political agenda and lifestyle which kept them dead and miserable in their sins. "Come to me," he said, "and I will give you freedom and vitality such as your movement would never dream and offer." He loved gays too much not to strike down a whitewashed wall.

- *Business*. Nathaniel asked, "Was economic wealth created for man, or man for economic wealth?" He called advertising a modern fusion of manipulation, propaganda, and porn, and took it to be the emblem of a mindset in which a business exists, not to serve customers, but to manipulate them into whatever will bring the most money into corporate coffers.

- *Consumers*. He accused them of entering into a sorceror's bargain to have wealth in our technology, being concerned with little as long as they had personal peace and affluence, and misusing wealth. He developed an argument, which I am not going to reproduce here, that both individual citizens and communities should take a good look at the Amish, not because they have a perfect solution, but because they are the one major group in America that does not automatically use every technology and service that comes out and that they can afford.

- *The tobacco industry*. To quote him: "You do something that kills people, for the mere purpose of obtaining profit. You are the largest assassins' guild in history."

- *Feminists*. His interactions with feminists were a little more complex than with some other groups, perhaps because of how deeply feminism has impacted not just a self-identified minority but the whole fabric of American culture, and because of how deeply he shared the concern of womens' status. Some of his remarks were flat-out incendiary. He said that, if feminism has to identify an enemy, a feminism that identified men as the enemy could be tolerable, but a feminism that identified non-feminist women as the enemy was inexcusable. "*Any* feminism worthy of the name," Nathaniel said, "*must* make the sisterhood of all women a central thesis." I think I saw him weeping over feminism more than any other group: when we talked, I began to see them through his eyes: not Rush Limbaugh-style feminazis, but lost sheep without a shepherd, women struggling to work against a curse and doomed to futility and backfire from the start, because they did not understand the nature of the curse, and so were like a doctor, giving higher and higher doses of medicine for the wrong condition, and wondering why the patient looked worse and worse. He tried to explain the remedy to that curse, and tried to explain it to a great many feminists — a few of them believed him, but the vast majority were offended.

- *Academia.* The most striking comment I remember him making was, "Hitler now stands as our culture's single most essential symbol of evil, not because he slaughtered six million Jews, but because he does not have any advocates left in academia. There is another ideology more vile than National Socialism, an ideology that exceeds the Nazi body count by a factor of ten and has made blood flow like a river in every single country where it has come into power. Its name is Marxism, and it is considered perfectly acceptable to be a Marxist in academia, a breeding ground of every heresy and intellectual filth our society has to offer."

- *Environmentalists.* To them, he said, "You have defiled a concern for God's earth not only with nature worship but also with racist, eugenic Malthusianism."

- *Media, especially television.* Most of what he said there were footnotes to Postman, Mander, and Muggeridge, and the rest wasn't that important.

- *Sensitivity police.* Nathaniel criticized them for "using gasoline to extinguish a fire."

- *The pro-choice forces.* Nathaniel criticized them for making a convenient redefinition of the boundaries of humanity and taking an attitude of "it's not really there if you can close your eyes to it." He said that on any biological perspective even, what grows inside a woman's womb is an organism of the species *homo sapiens,* and that the question of whether a fetus is human or unwanted tissue is a philosophical question only in the sense that whether a woman is human or just a convenient rape object is a philosophical question — that is, if you deliberately set out to make yourself stupider than you are and tarnish the name of philosophy by making it a smokescreen to hide what is obvious to common sense, then and only then can you satisfy yourself by saying "that is a philosophical question to which my answer is unwanted tissue." Nathaniel had other criticisms — one of them beginning by saying, "A real pro-choice scenario would be an undoubted improvement on the status quo," — but I do not wish to repeat them here.

- *The pro-life movement.* Nathaniel criticized them "for defending the sanctity of life from conception to natural birth."

Anyone who has not been offended by Nathaniel has failed to understand him.

There are many events which happened which I will not attempt to narrate. Nathaniel was healing people of all kinds of brokenness — physical, mental, emotional, spiritual. He had begun to teach us that he was giving us his authority — even over demons. He was explaining that he would need to die and rise from the dead, although none of us understood — or wanted to understand — what he was saying. And, through all of that, there were moments, precious, timeless moments, when we could have glimpses of who he was.

To begin explaining one of those moments, let me say that I am not affected by stage magic. It isn't just that I can (sometimes) see how a trick works; the actual illusion is only a tiny part of illusionism. It's indispensable, but it is unbelievably tiny — I know, because I was once an amateur magician, and I disappointed my audiences by performing an uninterrupted display of clever tricks that were nothing more. The real life's blood of a magic show is showmanship, something that is normally invisible: one of the marks of good showmanship is that the audience is oblivious to showmanship and instead wonders how on earth the magician did it. (It is incidentally true that, however much a good magic show makes audiences wonder "How did he do that?", a good magician *never* tells his audience how it happened. It's not protection of an initiate brotherhood's closely kept secrets — all such "secrets" are perfectly accessible to someone with a library card and a little spare time, just as the substitution-cipher-weak verification algorithm used for credit card numbers is available to anyone who can go to a search engine and type "mod10" in the query box — but basic entertainment principle: people who find out how magic tricks work are invariably disappointed. That is why I never tell other people how tricks at a magic show work, even when I do know; figuring out one or two minor tricks makes someone feel smug and clever, but knowing how the big trick worked simply ruins it.)

I have spoken as if showmanship's illusion is one-sided, as if it's all up to the magician. And it is, in a sense. But in another sense, it isn't. If I had been better as a stage magician and gotten farther, I would have experienced firsthand the difference between an audience that is excited, eager to see what is going on, or in high spirits, and one that is hostile, cranky with low blood sugar, or doesn't really want to be there. The illusion is not one-sided; it is the creation of both parties, performer and audience, the result of their cooperation — only the performer's cooperation is conscious and intentional, and the audience's cooperation is unconscious and unwitting.

There is something that happened with me, something that has broken the illusion by breaking my end of the creation — conscious uncooperation instead of unconscious cooperation — something that was closely related to my learning what is actually going on in television, and why I don't watch it. Now magic shows don't work on me. It's not that the illusion is broken because I can see how tricks work; rather, I see how tricks work because the illusion is broken. In Madeleine l'Engle's *A Wrinkle in Time*, on the nightmarish planet Camazotz, the man with red eyes gives Meg, Calvin, and Charles Wallace food. To Meg and Calvin it tastes like a wonderful turkey dinner. To Charles Wallace it tastes like wet sand. The man with red eyes can get into the chinks of Meg's mind, and Calvin's, enough to make an illusion mask how ghastly the food is. With Charles Wallace it doesn't work; the illusion doesn't work for him. I have been told I am very like Charles Wallace. I count it worthwhile that I am no longer automatically pulled by showmanship, particularly in an age where showmanship has taken a bloated role far beyond what any sane society would allow it. I count it my loss that I cannot now cooperate with the illusion even if I want to. (Nathaniel understands me on this score, and indeed has experienced the same awakening, but he can cooperate with the illusion. He also watches television for a couple of hours a month, only some of the time as a sociologist would.)

For these reasons, I was less than enthusiastic when Nathaniel showed me a flyer announcing a magic show for "children of all ages" in the bandstand at the park. I told him, "You go; I'll stay home and pray." He said, "Trust me."

We went about half an hour early. Parents were sitting in the bleachers, and kids were running about on the stage. We sat and talked for a few minutes, and then Nathaniel poked a little girl who was running by. She giggled, and he chased her on to the stage, and then started playing with another child, and another. He began to tell stories, ask questions, talk with them, hold them.

It seemed only a moment that the sky turned lavender and fireflies danced, and I looked down at my watch and realized that over an hour had passed. The magician never showed up, but not one of the children went home disappointed.

Whatever Nathaniel had, it was better than showmanship, better than illusion. He had a pull, a charisma, that drew people to him — something that arose out of the love that flowed in his heart. I am no longer drawn by television because television is fake, because television does a spectacular job of covering how empty its center was. Nathaniel wasn't like that. His charisma was an overflow of how full his center was. The meaning of this moment grew on me when I understood what moment it was, what time it was, that he had chosen to spend simply playing with children.

As the sky began to grow dark and mothers called their children home, I could begin to see — why hadn't I noticed it before? Nathaniel was afraid, and emotions of — what? expectation? imminence? trepidation? — were emotions that I could begin to feel as well. There was a sense that something important would happen. He purchased a loaf of bread and a bottle of wine, and called all of us to come into a deserted loft. We talked — really talked, about love, about too many things to mention, and then as there was a height of tension, he took the bread, and said, "Take this, and eat it. This is my body, which is broken for you. Do this in memory of me." Then he took the cup of wine, and said, "Take this, all of you, and drink. This is the new accord in my blood, poured out for the forgiveness of sins." Then he passed them around.

I talked with the others, years later; I was the only one who realized the significance of what was going on. There are still many people who have difficulty believing it, which is fine; there are a lot of things about Nathaniel that take a lot of believing. When I ate his body, I was taking, was drawn into, his community; when I drank his blood, I drank the divine life. The latter especially was precious to me in a way I cannot describe; I am a mystic, and there is something about the blood, hidden in the flesh, that... it is best not to talk too much about these things. I think some of them are things that it takes a child's heart to understand.

He asked us to be with him, not exactly to pray with him (although I am sure he also wanted that), but just to have the human presence of someone who loved him, perhaps just to have any human presence — and all I know I could think about was how long a day it had been, and how much I needed to get to sleep. We were awoken by a knock on the door, and Nathaniel looked at me — ooh! That look broke my heart. He did not say anything. He did not need to.

Nathaniel was shaking when he walked out in front of a veritable mob, and asked, "Who do you want?" Someone in the crowd said, "Nathaniel." He said, "I am the person you want. Get away from the building; you want me, not the others."

I was watching from the window, and I watched in stunned disbelief what the mob began doing to him. Then I climbed down, and ran as if there was no tomorrow. I had no shoes on, only socks, and when I collapsed, in exhaustion, my feet were bleeding.

Somehow (providence?) the others managed to find me, and we were huddling in a room, the doors locked, bolted, and barred with furniture, all shades drawn, glued to the TV, demoralized, defeated, in abject bewilderment. I had thrown up all I could, and felt sometimes dizzy, sometimes hot, sometimes nauseated, sometimes all three. I was leaning against the window, desparately praying that my head would stop spinning, and that if there were any way possible for Nathaniel to have survived that assault —

Someone knocked twice on the window, right next to my head, and my head cleared.

I was struck with terror, pulled back from the window, and prayed aloud that whoever it is would go away.

I heard Cassandra's voice loudly outside, saying, "It's me, Cassandra! I've seen Nathaniel! He's alive!"

I knew her voice, and my terror turned to rage, turned to what the damned call 'righteous indignation'. I said, "Of all the sick jokes, of all the unholy blows that the lowest schoolyard bully would not dream of stooping to," and poured out a stream of invective unlike any I have uttered before or since. I did not stop, did not even falter, when I heard her crying, nor when her tears turned to wailing. At the climax I said, "Unless Nathaniel stands before me, unless I feel the bones that have been crushed, I will never believe your sick joke."

I felt a tap on my shoulder, and when I turned around, Nathaniel looked into my eyes, gazing with both love and sorrow, and said, "Sean. I am here before you. Touch every one of my wounds." Then he touched me, and healed me of the sickness I had been feeling.

What could I do? I fell to the ground, and wept, and when I could stand I immediately left to go out and beg Cassandra's forgiveness. She forgave me — instantly. She gave me a hug, and said, "I had difficulty believing it, too.

You are forgiven." I can not tell the depths of love that are in that woman's heart. Then I returned, with Cassandra, and Nathaniel looked at me and said, "Sean, you are a metacultural, but you are also an American. What is real to you is largely what you have seen and what *The Skeptical Enquirer* says is real. You believe after having seen. God's blessing is on those who can rise above your culture's sin and believe these miracles without seeing."

Nathaniel said and did many other things, far too numerous for me to write down. I have not attempted a complete account, nor a representative account, nor even to cover all the bases. (Other writers have already done the last of those three.) Rather, I have written to show you the fresh power of Nathaniel's story, a story that is and will always be *here* and *now*. Do you understand him better?

The Monastery

It was late in the day, and my feet were hurting.

I had spent the past three hours on the winding path up the foothills, and you will excuse me if I was not paying attention to the beauty around me.

I saw it, and then wondered how I had not seen it—an alabaster palace rising out of the dark rock around it, hidden in a niche as foothill became mountain. After I saw it, I realized—I could not tell if the plants around me were wild or garden, but there was a grassy spot around it. Some of my fatigue eased as I looked into a pond and saw koi and goldfish swimming.

I looked around and saw the Gothic buildings, the trees, the stone path and walkways. I was beginning to relax, when I heard a voice say, "Good evening," and looked, and realized there was a man on the bench in front of me.

He was wearing a grey-green monk's robe, and cleaning a gun. He looked at me for a moment, tucked the gun into a shack, and welcomed me in.

Outside, the sun was setting. At the time, I thought of the last rays of the dying sun—but it was not that, so much as day giving birth to night. We passed inside to a hallway, with wooden chairs and a round wooden table. It seemed brightly enough lit, if by torchlight.

My guide disappeared into a hallway, and returned with

two silver chalices, and set one before me. He raised his chalice, and took a sip.

The wine was a dry white wine—refreshing and cold as ice. It must have gone to my head faster than I expected; I gave a long list of complaints, about how inaccessible this place was, and how hard the road. He listened silently, and I burst out, "Can you get the master of this place to come to me? I need to see him personally."

The servant softly replied, "He knows you are coming, and he will see you before you leave. In the mean time, may I show you around his corner of the world?"

I felt anger flaring within me; I am a busy man, and do not like to waste my time with subordinates. If it was only one of his underlings who would be available, I would have sent a subordinate myself. As I thought this, I was surprised to hear myself say, "Please."

We set down the chalices, and started walking through a maze of passageways. He took a small oil lamp, one that seemed to burn brightly, and we passed through a few doors before stepping into a massive room.

The room blazed with intense brilliance; I covered my eyes, and wondered how they made a flame to burn so bright. Then I realized that the chandaliers were lit with incandescent light. The shelves had illuminated manuscripts next to books with plastic covers—computer science next to bestiaries. My guide went over by one place, tapped with his finger—and I realized that he was at a computer.

Perhaps reading the look on my face, my guide told me, "The master uses computers as much as you do. Do you need to check your e-mail?"

I asked, "Why are there torches in the room you left me in, and electric light here?"

He said, "Is a person not permitted to use both? The master, as you call him, believes that technology is like alcohol—good within proper limits—and not something you have to use as much as you can. There are electric lights here because their brilliance makes reading easier on the eyes. Other rooms have torches, or nothing at all, because a flame has a different meaning, one that we prefer. Never mind; I can get you a flashlight if you like. Oh, and you can take off your watch now. It won't work here."

"It won't work? Look, it keeps track of time to the second, and it is working as we speak!"

The man studied my watch, though I think he was humoring me, and said, "It will give a number as well here as anywhere else. But that number means very little here, and you would do just as well to put it in your pocket."

I looked at my watch, and kept it on. He asked, "What time is it?"

I looked, and said, "19:58."

"Is that all?"

I told him the seconds, and then the date and year, and added, "But it doesn't feel like the 21st century here." I was beginning to feel a little nervous.

He said, "What century do you think it is here?"

I said, "Like a medieval time that someone's taken a scissors to. You have a garden with perfect gothic architecture, and you in a monk's robe, holding an expensive-looking rifle. And a computer in a library that doesn't even try to organize books by subject or time."

I looked around on the wall, and noticed a hunting trophy. Or at least that's what I took it for at first. There was a large sheild-shaped piece of wood, such as would come with a beautiful stag—but no animal's head. Instead, there were hundreds upon hundreds of bullet holes in the wood— enough that the wood should have shattered. I walked over, and read the glass plate: "This magnificent deer shot 1-4-98 in Wisconsin with an AK-47. God bless the NRA."

I laughed a minute, and said, "What is this doing in here?"

The servant said, "What is anything doing here? Does it surprise you?"

I said, "From what I have heard, the master of this place

is very serious about life."

My guide said, "Of course he is. And he cherishes laughter."

I looked around a bit, but could not understand why the other things were there—only be puzzled at how anyone could arrange a computer and other oddments to make a room that felt unmistably medieval. Or was it? "What time is it here? To you?"

My guide said, "Every time and no time. We do not measure time by numbers here; to the extent that time is 'measured', we 'measure' by what fills it—something qualitative and not quantiative. Your culture measures a place's niche in history by how many physical years have passed before it; we understand that well enough, but we reckon time, not by its place in the march of seconds, but by the content of its character. You may think of this place as medieval if you want; others view it as ancient, and not a small part is postmodern—more than the computer is contemporary."

I looked at my watch. Only five minutes had passed. I felt frustration and puzzlement, and wondered how long this could go on.

"When can we move on from here?"

"When you are ready. You aren't ready yet."

I looked at my watch. Not even ten seconds had passed. The second hand seemed to be moving very slowly.

I felt something moving in the back of my mind, but I tried to push it back. The second hand continued on its lazy journey, and then—I took off my watch and put it in my pocket.

My guide stood up and said, "Walk this way, please."

He led me to a doorway, opening a door, and warning me not to step over the threshold. I looked, and saw why—there was a drop of about a foot, into a pool of water. The walls were blue, and there was sand at the far end. Two children—a little boy and a little girl—were making sand castles.

He led me through the mazelike passages to rooms I cannot describe. One room had mechanical devices in all stages of assembly and disassembly. Another was bare and clean. The kitchen had pepperoni and peppers hanging, and was filled with an orange glow that was more than torchlight. There was a deserted classroom filled with flickering blue light, and then we walked into a theatre.

The chamber was small, and this theatre had more than the usual slanted floor. The best way I could describe it is to say that it was a wall, at times vertical, with handholds and outcroppings. There were three women and two men on the stage, but not standing—or sitting, for that matter. They were climbing, shifting about as they talked.

I could not understand their language, but there was something about it that fascinated me. I was surprised to find myself listening to it. I was even more surprised to realize that, if I could not understand the words, I could no less grasp the story. It was a story of friendship, and there is something important in that words melted into song, and climbing into dance.

I watched to the end. The actors and actresses did not disappear backstage, but simply climbed down into the audience, and began talking with people. I could not tell if the conversation was part of the act, or if they were just seeing friends. I wondered if it really made any difference—and then realized, with a flash, that I had caught a glimpse into how this place worked.

When I wanted to go, the servant led me to a room filled with pipes. He cranked a wheel, and I heard gears turning, and began to see the jet black keys of an organ. He played a musical fragment; it sounded incomplete.

He said, "Play."

I closed my eyes and said, "I don't know how to play any instrument."

He repeated the fragment and said, "That doesn't matter. Play."

There followed a game of question and answer—he

would improvise a snatch of music, and I would follow. I would say that it was beautiful, but I couldn't really put it that way. It would be better to say that his music was mediocre, and mine didn't quite reach that standard.

We walked out into a cloister. I gasped. There was a sheltered pathway around a grassy court and a pool stirred by fish. It was illumined by moon and star, and the brilliance was dazzling.

We walked around, and I looked. In my mind's eye I could see white marble statues of saints praying—I wasn't sure, but I made up my mind to suggest that to the master. After a time we stopped walking on the grass, and entered another door.

Not too far into the hallway, he turned, set the oil lamp into a small alcove, and began to rise up the wall. Shortly before disappearing into the blackness above, he said, "Climb."

I learn a little, I think. I did not protest; I put my hands and feet on the wall, and felt nothing. I leaned against it, and felt something give way—something yielding to give a handhold. Then I started climbing. I fell a couple of times, but reached the shadows where he disappeared. He took me by the hand and began to lead me along a path.

I could feel a wall on either side, and then nothing, save his hand and my feet. Where was I? I said, "I can't see!"

A woman's voice said, "No one can see here. Eyes aren't needed." I felt an arm around my waist, and a gentle squeeze.

I felt that warmth, and said, "I came to this place because I wanted to see the master of this house, and I wanted to see him personally. Now—I am ready to leave without seeing him. I have seen enough, and I no longer want to trouble him."

I felt my guide's hand on my shoulder, and heard his voice as he said, "You have seen me personally, and you are not troubling me. You are here at my invitation. You will always be welcome here."

When I first entered the house, I would have been stunned. Now, it seemed the last puzzle piece in something I had been gathering since I started hiking.

The conversation was deep, and I cannot tell you what was said. I don't mean that I forgot it—I remember it clearly enough. I don't really mean that it would be a breach of confidence—it might be that as well. What I mean is that there was something special in that room, and it would not make much sense to you even if I could explain it. If I were to say that we talked in a room without light, where you had to feel around to move about—it would be literally true, but beside the point. When I remember the room, I do not think about what wasn't there, but what was there. I was glad I took off my watch—but I cannot say why. The best thing I can say is that if you can figure out how a person could be aware of a succession of moments, and at the same time have time sense that is not entirely linear—or at very least not *just* linear—you have a glimpse of what I found in that room.

We talked long, and it was late into the next day when I got up from a perfectly ordinary guestroom, packed, and left. I put on my watch, returned to my business, and started working on the backlog of invoices and meetings that accumulated in my absence. I'm still pretty busy, but I have never left that room.

A Strange Picture

As I walked through the gallery, I immediately stopped when I saw one painting. As I stopped and looked at it, I became more and more deeply puzzled. I'm not sure how to describe the picture.

It was a picture of a city, viewed from a high vantage point. It was a very beautiful city, with houses and towers and streets and parks. As I stood there, I thought for a moment that I heard the sound of children playing—and I looked, but I was the only one present.

This made all the more puzzling the fact that it was a disturbing picture—chilling even. It was not disturbing in the sense that a picture of the Crucifixion is disturbing, where the very beauty is what makes it disturbing. I tried to see what part might be causing it, and met frustration. It seemed that the beauty was itself what was wrong—but that couldn't be right, because when I looked more closely I saw that the city was even more beautiful than I had imagined. The best way I could explain it to myself was that the ugliness of the picture could not exist except for an inestimable beauty. It was like an unflattering picture of an attractive friend—you can see your friend's good looks, but the picture shows your friend in an ugly way. You have to fight the picture to really see your friend's beauty—and I realized that I was fighting the picture to see the city's real beauty. It was a shallow picture of something profound, and it was perverse. An artist who paints a picture helps you to see through his eyes—most help you to see a beauty that you could not see if you were standing in the same spot and looking. This was like looking at a mountaintop through a pair of eyes that were blind, with a blindness far more terrible, far more crippling, than any blindness that is merely physical. I stepped back in nausea.

I leaned against a pillar for support, and my eyes fell to the bottom of the frame. I glanced on the picture's title: *Porn*.

Hysterical Friction: A Medievalist Jibe at Disney Princess Videos

From Falstaff to Herodotus, grace: I send your excellence my manuscript, as revised again, and have returned the Imaginarium. I have tried to envision what life was really like in The Setting, but yet also keep things contemporary. Please send my boots and cloak by my nephew.

Here is the story:

Oct 8, 2020, Anytown, USA.

Anna looked at the sky. The position of the sun showed that it was the ninth hour, and from the clouds it looked like about four or five hours until there would be a light rain.

She stood reverently and attentively, pulled out her iPhone, and used a pirated Internet Explorer 6 app to spend deliberate time on social networks: first Facebook, then Twitter, then Amazon. It was the last that offered the richest social interaction.

Technology in that society underscored the sacred and interlocking rhythm and time, with its cycles of lifetime, year, month, and day, right down to the single short hour. But there was a lot of technology, and it had changed things. The road had for ages been shared between pedestrian man and horse. Now, decades after automobiles had taken root, it had to be shared between man, horse, and motorcar. A shiny, dark Ford Ferrari raced by her on the sidewalk. She paused to contemplate its beauty. Then she listened, entranced, as a poor street musician played sad, sad music on a Honda Accordion.

And in all this she was human. Neither her lord nor she knew how many winters each had passed when they married; neither her lord nor she for that matter knew that it was the twentieth century. She cared for birth and mirth, and she loved her little ones. She did not know how many winters old they were, either. And there was life within her.

And she was intensely religious, and intensely superstitious, so far as to be almost entirely tacit. She knew the stories of the saints, and attended church a few times a year. She lived long under religion's shadow. And her mind was tranquil, unhurried, unworried, and this without the slightest effort to learn Antarctican Mindfulness.

And in all this, she was *content*. Her family had lived on the same sandlot; more than seven generations had been born, lived, and died without traveling twenty miles from this root. The stones and herbs were family to her as much as men, but this was, again, tacit.

She was human. Really and truly human, no matter what others thought the epoch was.

Then a crow crowed. She looked around, thoughtfully. It was well nigh time to visit her sister.

"*But how to get there?*" she thought, and then, "I have walked in the opposite direction, and she will be upset if I am even *two or three* hours late."

Then a solution occurred to her. She reached into her pocket, pulled out her new iPhone Pro, pulled up the Uber app, and ordered a shared ride.

Unashamed

The day his daughter Abigail was born was the best day of Abraham's life. Like father, like daughter, they said in the village, and especially of them. He was an accomplished musician, and she breathed music.

He taught her a music that was simple, pure, powerful. It had only one voice; it needed only one voice. It moved slowly, unhurriedly, and had a force that was spellbinding. Abraham taught Abigail many songs, and as she grew, she began to make songs of her own. Abigail knew nothing of polyphony, nor of hurried technical complexity; her songs needed nothing of them. Her songs came from an unhurried time out of time, gentle as lapping waves, and mighty as an ocean.

One day a visitor came, a young man in a white suit. He said, "Before your father comes, I would like you to see what you have been missing." He took out a music player, and began to play.

Abby at first covered her ears; she was in turn stunned, shocked, and intrigued. The music had many voices, weaving in and out of each other quickly, intricately. She heard wheels within wheels within wheels within wheels of complexity. She began to try, began to think in polyphony — and the man said, "I will come to you later. It is time for your music with your father."

Every time in her life, sitting down at a keyboard with her father was the highlight of her day. Every day but this day. This day, she could only think about how simple and plain the music was, how lacking in complexity. Abraham stopped his song and looked at his daughter. "Who have you been listening to, Abigail?"

Something had been gnawing at Abby's heart; the music seemed bleak, grey. It was as if she had beheld the world in fair moonlight, and then a blast of eerie light assaulted her eyes — and now she could see nothing. She felt embarrassed by her music, ashamed to have dared to approach her father with anything so terribly unsophisticated. Crying, she gathered up her skirts and ran as if there were no tomorrow.

Tomorrow came, and the day after; it was a miserable day, after sleeping in a gutter. Abigail began to beg, and it was over a year before another beggar let her play on his keyboard. Abby learned to play in many voices; she was so successful that she forgot that she was missing something. She occupied herself so fully with intricate music that in another year she was asked to give concerts and performances. Her music was rich and full, and her heart was poor and empty.

Years passed, and Abigail gave *the* performance of her career. It was before a sold-out audience, and it was written about in the papers. She walked out after the performance and the reception, with moonlight falling over soft grass and fireflies dancing, and something happened.

Abby heard the wind blowing in the trees.

In the wind, Abigail heard music, and in the wind and the music Abigail heard all the things she had lost in her childhood. It was as if she had looked in an image and asked, "What is that wretched thing?" — and realized she was looking into a mirror. No, it was not quite that; it was as if in an instant her whole world was turned upside down, and her musical complexity she could not bear. She heard all over again the words, "Who have you been listening to?"

— only, this time, she did not think them the words of a jealous monster, but words of concern, words of "Who has struck a blow against you?" She saw that she was blind and heard that she was deaf: that the hearing of complexity had not simply been an opening of her ears, but a wounding, a smiting, after which she could not know the concentrated presence a child had known, no matter how complex — or how simple — the music became. The sword cut deeper when she tried to sing songs from her childhood, at first could remember none, then could remember one — and it sounded empty — and she knew that the song was not empty. It was her. She lay down and wailed.

Suddenly, she realized she was not alone. An old man was watching her. Abigail looked around in fright; there was nowhere to run to hide. "What do you want?" she said.

"There is music even in your wail."

"I loathe music."

There was a time of silence, a time that drew uncomfortably long, and Abigail asked, "What is your name?"

The man said, "Look into my eyes. You know my name."

Abigail stood, poised like a man balancing on the edge of a sword, a chasm to either side. She did not — Abigail shrieked with joy. "*Daddy!*"

"It has been a long time since we've sat down at music, sweet daughter."

"You don't want to hear my music. I was ashamed of what we used to play, and I am now ashamed of it all."

"Oh, child! Yes, I do. *I will never be ashamed of you.* Will you come and walk with me? I have a keyboard."

As Abby's fingers began to dance, she first felt as if she were being weighed in the balance and found wanting. The self-consciousness she had finally managed to banish in her playing was now there — ugly, repulsive — and then she was through it. She made a horrible mistake, and then another, and then laughed, and Abraham laughed with her. Abby began to play and then sing, serious, inconsequential, silly, and delightful in the presence of her father. It was as if shackles fell from her wrists, her tongue loosed — she thought for a moment that she was like a little girl again, playing at her father's side, and then knew that it was better. What could she compare it to? She couldn't. She was at a simplicity beyond complexity, and her father called forth from her music that she could never have done without her trouble. The music seemed like dance, like laughter; it was under and around and through her, connecting her with her father, a moment out of time.

After they had both sung and laughed and cried, Abraham said, "Abby, will you come home with me? My house has never been the same without you."

The Voyage

I

He kicked the can, which skittered across the sidewalk. Shards of glass bounced off, their razor sharp edges gleaming in the light. Jason sat down on a park bench, and glared at the old man sitting on the other end. He looked decrepit and stupid, with a moronic smile. The man was feeding pigeons. The geezer probably didn't even own a TV. A boring man doing a boring thing in a boring place on a boring day.

Jason liked to verbally spar with people. He liked to free them from their deceptions, their illusions. "The unexamined life is not worth living," and he would rather be hated as a gadfly than loved as a demagogue.

As Jason sat thinking, the old man said, "It's a beautiful, sunny day, isn't it?"

"The Poet Wordsworth aptly called it 'the dreary light of common day.' It is a dull surface, under which ferments a world of evil. Did you know, for instance, that Hitler's Holocaust was only one of many massive genocides this century that killed over a million people? Did you know that even Hitler's Jews are dwarfed by the fifty million who died in Stalin's purges?"

The smile disappeared from the old man's face. "No, I did not."

"You who say that it's a beautiful day — what do you know about suffering?"

The old man's face quivered, ever so slightly, for a moment. "My best friend, when I was a boy, was named Abraham. He died at Auschwitz. My eldest brother, on the other hand, was swept up by the Nazi propaganda and became a concentration camp guard. He was never convicted of war crimes, but he hanged himself a week after I was married. I am now a widower."

Jason was silent for a moment. He was struck with respect at this man's suffering — and watched as a tear gathered in his eyes, and slowly trickled down his wrinkled cheek. As he looked, he saw part of why the old man looked so ugly to him — his face bore scars of chemical burns.

A sense of discomfort and unease began to fill the young man. He shifted slightly, and began to talk about something else.

"I have read many books about knights and ladies, about wizards and dragons. In those stories, there is magic and wonder; there are fairies who grant wishes. The hero wins, and the story is beautiful. This world is so bleak and desolate and gray next to those worlds. If only there were another world. If only there were a way to get in."

"How do you know that there isn't?"

The young man looked with puzzlement. "What do you mean?"

"How do you know that this fantasy isn't true?"

"I have never had any reason to believe in it."

"When you were a little boy, did you believe in the Holocaust?"

"I hadn't even heard of it, let alone having reason to believe in it."

"But was it true?"

The young man looked as if he was about to answer, and then said, "Do you really believe in another world, in magic and wonder?"

"I might."

"Tell me about it."

"I cannot now explain it in any words that would make sense to you. I could try, but it would sound like complete nonsense."

"Try."

"Pretend that I am blind. Explain to me the colors."

Jason opened his mouth, paused for a second, and then closed it.

"Am I to believe that you are some sort of great wizard, and that you have a gift of seeing into and travelling to another world?"

"Maybe."

The old man spoke in enigmas and riddles, and yet there was something about him... He did not seem to be lying — and if he was, he was a far better liar than most. He was a puzzle, and Jason liked puzzles. He had been tricked and manipulated many times, and it might at least break the tedium to be tricked and manipulated by someone who was more interesting than he looked. So he decided to play along.

"Do you think that I could make my way into another world?"

"Maybe."

"Is it hard?"

"It is very hard, and very easy. How much do you want to do it?"

"Very much."

"If I send you on great and difficult tests, to meet many trials, will you do it?"

"I will."

"If I tell you to spend long hours studying spell books and grimoires, finding potions and amulets, are you ready for that?"

"I am."

"And if I set before you tasks more difficult and strange,

and send you to do battles against monsters more evil than assassins and more deadly than dragons, can you do that?"

"I will try."

"Can you trust me?"

For a moment, Jason's mask slipped. He stalled. A minute passed — a minute that seemed like a year. Finally, he croaked, "I don't know."

The old man nodded, and said, "I understand." He looked at the young man; there was something in his eyes that the young man could not identify.

"The way is difficult, with many trials, and the last one is the most difficult of them all. I cannot tell you what they will all be like, or even their number. When we next meet, I will be ready to give you the first."

"When do you want to meet next?"

"No matter when; we will meet."

"Can you help me?"

"I cannot do your tasks for you. But I give you this."

The old man placed his hand on the young man's head, his palm atop the skull, fingers and thumb spreading out across his scalp. He closed his eyes — and Jason felt that it would be proper to do the same. He sat in absolute silence and stillness. A moment passed.

Finally the old man removed his hand. Picking up his cane, he stood up, and slowly began to walk away, leaving Jason sitting and pondering.

II

The next day, doubts filled Jason's mind. Had he dreamed the encounter? Why would there be such a bizarre old man? If he really had the powers and knew the wonders he hinted at, why on earth would he be sitting in a park and feeding pigeons? Each city had its share of eccentrics, but still...

As he went about his studies and activities for the next few days, he was nagged by thoughts about the man. He loved fantasy, from childhood games of make-believe to reading books and watching movies — but all of his yearning would not make it com true. He felt that he could neither believe nor trust the old man. Yet their interaction had excited, not quite a hope, but at least a desire that it could be true. He believed in fairies as a child, and he wondered if there might be a time to believe in fairies again.

He didn't talk with anyone about it; others would probably think him a fool. He was sitting in a diner, sipping a cup of coffee and pondering, when a familiar voice said, "May I join you?"

He looked up, startled, and then said, "Please." As the old man sat down, Jason asked, "I forgot to ask your name."

"Senex. And yours?"

"Jason."

"The name of a hero, if I am remembering my mythology correctly," Senex said.

Jason had been thinking of how dull and common his name sounded next to 'Senex', and was again slightly startled. The man still looked old, wrinkled, and ugly — and yet there now seemed to be the faintest hint of something regal about his appearance. After a time, Jason asked, "Do you really have quests for me?"

"Yes, I do. They will help prepare you to enter, and receive the gift and the power."

"And what is the first?"

Senex reached, with both hands, into his pocket. He moved his hands for a little while, as if grasping something slippery, and then brought forth a loosely closed hand. He held his hand over the table, and opened it.

"What do you see?"

"I see nothing. Your hand is empty."

"Do you really see nothing in my hand?"

"Nothing."

"Look closer."

"I still see nothing."

"Wait."

Senex turned his hand, slowly, slightly, from side to side. At last, a tiny gleam of light caught Jason's eye. He immediately bent over to look more closely.

"What do you see?"

"I see a tiny grain of sand."

"Take it."

Jason picked up the grain of sand, and looked at it for a second. "What is my first quest?"

"You have already embarked on your first quest."

"When will I be done?"

"I don't know."

The old man stood up, and walked out of the diner.

III

Back in his room, Jason took the grain of sand out of the napkin he had wrapped it in, and placed in on a white handkerchief on his desk.

It was small, and barely visible. It did not quite look the yellow of beaches — more like a tiny, oddly shaped pebble.

He pulled out a pin, and began to push it about. It rolled irregularly, like a tiny football. As it turned about, it gleamed every now and then. He pulled out a magnifying glass through which to look at it. Magnified, it appeared a small, bulbous crystal, which turned light and dark as it rolled over the fibers of the cloth.

"I wonder if..." He wrapped it up and went to a jeweler, to see if it might be a diamond or some other precious stone.

He came back, disappointed. It was sand, the same as untold numbers of other grains on beaches and in children's sand boxes. It puzzled him. Was it more precious than diamond, a key to a magical portal? It did not scream out, "I am magical!"; it did not glow in the dark, or levitate in the air, or shock him as he touched it. If there was something special about it, it was more subtle than that. But how would Jason unlock the secret? Time passed, and he began to doubt that there was any secret at all — that it was anything more than a common grain of sand.

It was in one of these moments of doubt that he again encountered Senex in the diner, drinking a cup of coffee.

"I don't get it," Jason said, sitting down. Senex still looked into his coffee, sipping it. "What don't you get?"

"You hint at a world of wonders, and then give me a common grain of sand. Are you playing games with me?"

Senex set down his coffee, and looked into Jason's eyes. "What do you think?"

Jason looked at the old man. He began to open his mouth, and then swallowed. "I cannot say that you seem cruel, but neither can I say that your words and actions make any sense to me."

"And?"

After Jason said nothing, the old man said, "What were you looking for?"

"Something great. Something awesome. Something mysterious. A storm of light, maybe. Turgid forces. Ritual magic."

"And what did you find?"

"A common grain of sand."

"Is that all?"

Jason pulled the napkin from his pocket, and unfolded the grain of sand. "All I see is a common grain of sand. Maybe there is something else, but it is invisible to me." He looked at the old man in puzzlement, and saw a look of knowledge in Senex's eyes. "Can you see something else, something that is invisible to me?"

"I can."

"What?"

"Tell me everything that you know about it. What is it?"

"It is something that is found on beaches."

"That is where it is found. What is it?"

"It is an odd-shaped, bulbous thing, very tiny."

"That is its size and shape. What is it?"

"The jeweler said that it is not diamond, or quartz, or

anything else like that."

"That is what it is not. What is it?"

"The jeweler said that it is a crystal of silicon and oxygen atoms."

"That is its scientific structure and constituency. What is it?"

"Is it all of these things?"

"All of these things are true of it. What is it?"

Jason drew a deep breath and said, "I don't know."

"Make it into a rabbit."

"How am I supposed to do that?"

"If you can't do that, make it into something else. A fish, perhaps."

"I can't."

"Destroy it."

Jason placed the grain of sand between a knife and a spoon, and crushed it to dust.

"You have broken it into smaller pieces. Now destroy it."

Jason dropped the spoon and knife; the fragments that were the grain of sand, settled on the table. "I can't."

"What is it?"

"I don't know." Jason looked into the old man's eyes, expecting to see a look of sadistic pleasure. Instead, he saw the look of greatest compassion.

Jason said, "It is a mystery."

The old man smiled.

Jason gathered the fragments into his napkin, and walked away.

IV

Jason began to think about stones and crystals. The exquisitely rare crystals, the diamond as their queen, were prized, not only because they were beautiful, but because they were rare. Quartz and other crystals, in their luminous beauty, were no surprise to be said to be magical. So it was not too surprising that there should also be a hidden, tiny beauty to the stone and crystal commonly called a grain of sand. Few people owned these gems, not because they were hidden deep within the earth, but because they were hidden from people's notice. When entering another world, Jason would like to be ready to appreciate its beauty — and who knows? Perhaps sand was a treasure imported en masse from that world. In the mean time, he would enjoy his newfound crystalline treasure.

V

Jason asked Senex, "Am I prepared to enter another world, the world from which crystals come?"

Senex answered, "You have begun to begin."

Jason asked, "Are there wonders which make sand pale in comparison?"

Senex answered, "There are wonders which make sand look very bright by the light they shine on it."

VI

Senex lit a candle. Jason watched, waiting for an explanation.

The flame danced and spun. It filled the white column of wax beneath it with a soft glow that melted into the darkness. The flame itself, divided into tongues, danced and jumped again and again into the air, looking as if it just might fly. All around, it illuminated the surrounding forms with a golden light; shadows loomed on the walls and melted into the surroundings.

As Jason watched, a thin layer of clear, molten wax began to form atop the candle. As the flame burned, the heat began to seep into the wax, and the tiny pool grew deeper. A drop, like a tear, began to form on one side of the pool. The molten wax flowed, the stream carrying an indentation in the top of the wax column. The flame jumped and blazed, then settled down as, one by one, drops of molten wax trickled down the side.

The candle was tapered and thin, and it seemed to Jason only a minute until it burned all the way down, and a tiny red glow in the wick rested at the base of an ascending, twisting, turning stream of wispy smoke. Jason sat in peace, enjoying a sense of calm and fullness, digesting the beauty he had watched.

Senex's voice broke the silence. "You have passed your second test, Jason."

VII

The old man had helped Jason open his eyes to one part of the natural world, and he began to explore, with the wonder of a child, the magic all around him.

He discovered that there was one type of item which was the easiest thing in the world to cut with a knife — but, as soon as you had cut it, the cut would instantly heal; there it would be, as whole as ever! It would shape itself around whatever you put it in, and could squeeze through even the tiny holes in cloth — but he had to be careful, because it would also climb the cloth like a ladder. It was quite mischievous — there were some things, which resembled grains of sound, which it would take and make completely invisible.

There were other things that would hide behind, and yet mimic the people and the trees. They were like marionettes, except that they exaggerated and distorted the profiles of whatever they were making fun of. They also played hide and seek with the light, and were very quick — whenever the light would peek to see if it would find them, they would already be hidden somewhere else.

He saw great, massive citadels with vaults beneath, storing hoards of gold and gems deep within, under protections that a dragon's fire could not scratch. Those citadels were decorated, so that even those who dare not break in, would yet come and visit, seeing the gay streamers and the skittish sentinels.

There was another creature that Jason could not see, but was forever sneaking up and tackling him. It never knocked him over, but always wanted to play — it would tousle people's hair, and tickle the little children. It played with the other creatures, too — it jumped around on the grass, and danced and spun with the leaves.

There were other strange creatures that skittered around timidly — some jumped along the ground; some climbed trees and buildings; some swam like fish through the air. Most fled at his approach, but a few would let him touch them — and they were soft and warm.

Even greater than his joy at this beauty was a sense that, beautiful as these things were, they also hinted at something else, a deeper magic. Jason tried to see what it might be, but it always eluded him.

VIII

Enthralled as he was, Jason could not shut out a sense that the beauty was not alone — that there was also something dark and perverse as well. With such beauty, Jason thought in his most enthralled moments that this surely must be the best of all possible worlds. But they he was shocked by ugly realities that forced themselves upon his consciousness: robberies and rapes, children being treated cruelly, and children treating others cruelly. The beauty made him feel as if, somehow, if he opened his eyes wide enough to see all the beauty there was, everything would be perfect — but, try as he might, it didn't work. It was like smelling the softest lilac fragrance on the breeze — and then being punched in the stomach.

It was sinking into a darker mood that he again met Senex, this time on a street littered with garbage. He greeted the old man harshly: "Wave your magic wand, old man, and make this refuse turn into flowers. Open my eyes, so that I may see that all suffering is an illusion, that we live in the best of all possible worlds."

"Suffering is not an illusion, and we do not live in the best of all possible worlds."

"What of the world you said I had begun preparing to enter? Is it not an escape from suffering?"

"Do you not remember the very first question you asked me? Do you not remember the answer?" Tears began to gather in Senex's eyes.

Jason savored a thrill of pleasure at watching the old man suffer, and knowing that the same darkness tormented them both. Then he realized what he was doing, and felt a sense of shame and revulsion at himself. He hated himself and the old man for what he felt.

"If you were going to attack a dragon," the old man finally began, "would you rush at it with neither weapon nor armor nor training? Or would you take at least a little preparation before setting out to attack a leviathan that has slain many heroes far greater than yourself?"

Jason said nothing.

"The questions you ask are big questions, and they must be faced. I wrestle with them, too. And I fear. I do not blame you at all for asking them, though your attitude in asking pierces me." A tear trickled down Senex's cheek.

Jason felt a black hole of shame inside his heart. The darkness he saw, and hated in the world around him — Jason now realized that it was inside him, too. It was like a worm, attacking from outside, and gnawing from within.

He wanted to die.

"Jason," the old man's voice said. "Jason, look at me."

Jason stared at the ground.

"Please."

Jason looked up and cringed, expecting a storm of fury. He looked up, waiting for his punishment. But his gaze was met by teary eyes — and compassion.

"I forgive you."

IX

It was with a certain heaviness that Jason awaited the coming lessons. Not that they doubted that they were good — he was sure of that. But up ahead loomed a fierce battle. The worst part of it was that he knew that the enemy, the worm, was not only lurking at large. It was also inside his heart.

Yet dark as the darkness was, it could never put the light out. And Senex was showing him new things at each meeting.

Senex had with him a book. He said, "Close your eyes and imagine." He opened its dusty leaves, and began to read:

"You pull your arms to your side and glide through the water. On your left is a fountain of bubbles, upside down, beneath a waterfall; the bubbles shoot down and then cascade out and to the surface. To your right swims a school of colorful fish, red and blue with thin black stripes. The water is cool, and you can feel the currents gently pushing and pulling on your body. Ahead of you, seaweed above and long, bright green leaves below wave back and forth, flowing and bending. You pull your arms, again, with a powerful stroke which shoots you forward under the seaweed; your back feels cool in the shade. You kick, and you feel the warmth of the sun again, soaking in and through your skin and muscles. Bands of light dance on the sand beneath you, as the light is bent and turned by the waves."

Senex began to lead Jason through mathematics, history, philosophy, literature — and Jason began to behind a new and different beauty, a beauty that cannot be seen with the eye, nor touched with the hand, but only grasped with the mind. He began to explore imagination, and ideas, and metaphors. He saw light dance in the poetry Senex read; he saw the beauty of order and reason in the philosophers Senex cited. The connections, the play, the dance of ideas was wonderful. Together they explored ideas, and it was an awesome beauty. Jason had a razor sharp mind, and he began to make connections that surprised even Senex.

X

"I still wish that I were a fairy," Jason said, "or that I could become one."

"What do you think you are?"

A searing pain, a pain of dark memory, flashed through Jason's soul. "I don't know," he said. "I hate myself."

"Do you believe that there are some things for everyone to enjoy?"

"Of course. You have shown me what I was blind to — that, outside of us, there are rocks, and stars, and the sky, and trees, and blades of grass, and snails, and stags, and chipmunks, and fish, and eagles, and logs, and mountains, and clouds, and wind, and rain, and the moon, and silence, and music, and beauty, and artwork, and poetry, and stories, and theorems, and arguments, and logic, and intuition, and laughter, and happiness, and books, and subtlety, and metaphors, and words, and st—"

Senex cut him off. "Do you believe that any of it has been given specifically to you?"

Jason looked down at his feet.

"What are you looking at, Jason?"

Jason mumbled, "My feet."

"What are your feet?"

"I don't know," he said, pausing for a moment. Then he continued, "I don't know where they are from, but they move about at my command, like two strange servants, carrying me wherever I want to go."

"What do they carry?"

"A house that has eyes to see, and hands to let me touch and move things, and innards that support and let me live." He paused for a second, and then said, "It is a clockwork masterpiece."

"What lives in this house."

"Well, there is at least a mind that can learn, and think, and explore, and feel."

"Is that rubbish?"

Jason begrudgingly admitted, "No."

"Jason, why are you so downcast?"?

"Because that is not all. Because there is a worm. It roams the world, and it lives deep inside of me."

"I know."

Jason drew back in fear. "What are you going to do to me?"

"What do you think?"

"You must hate me."

"I hate the worm inside of you with all my heart. But I do not hate you."

"You don't?"

"Jason, I love you."

Jason looked up. His face quivered, and tears began to slide down his cheeks. "You do?"

"Jason, may I give you a hug?"

Jason nodded his head.

The tears flowed from deep within. They were tears of sorrow, but yet they were different from the bitter tears he had fought before. They were painful, yet also tears of cleansing and healing.

XI

"In the stories I read, I believe that there are people like us, and also strange and wonderful people like fairies, and elves, and dwarves, and gnomes. I wish I could know them."

"I believe that there are people like us, and also strange and wonderful people like blacks and Hispanics and Asians and Native Americans. And I count myself the richer for the friendships I have shared with such people."

Senex paused, and then continued. "I believe that you have seen much of the beauty that can be perceived with the body and with the mind, and also that you are beginning to appreciate your body and mind — yes, I know that you still wonder why they were given you. You are close to being ready to enter the other world now.

Jason suddenly looked up. "There's more?"

"There is much more, my friend. I think that you are ready for the last trial before entering. The challenge is this: that you must make a friend."

"So I can enter after I make a friend?"

"Yes, but you can't make a friend in order to get in. You must make a friend for the sake of making a friend.

"Does it matter which race?"

"It matters a great deal, but not in the way that you are thinking. You will be blessed by a friend of any race; the difference is not the amount of blessing, but what kind."

XII

Jason was walking along a sidewalk, and saw some children playing in the street, kicking a ball around. Then he watched in horror

a truck comes along
a child kicks the ball
a little girl runs after it
in front of the car
girl trips
brakes screech

Time seemed to slow down; Jason watched everything in horrible slowness.

Then Jason realized he was lying on his side, on the opposite sidewalk. The little girl was in his arms, screaming and holding her knee. The ball was still in the street — flat as a pancake.

Adults began to come out of the building. A young woman ran over to the girl, yelling, "My baby!"

An older woman, with wrinkled walnut skin and silvery hair, walked up to him and said, "Son, you wanna come in?

You bleedin'."

Jason looked down. There was a rough abrasion on his elbow, and his shoulder hurt.

Inside the apartment, he was in the same room as the little girl. Her mother was gently wiping her skinned knee with a warm, wet washcloth; the girl was screaming bloody murder. He also had a cloth washing over his elbow; it stung sharply. The children had come in, and were simultaneously and very quickly trying to explain what happened.

The chaos subsided; the children were calmed, and (the children speaking more slowly, and one at a time) the adults understood what happened. "You gonna be soah t'marrah" — and he was.

The family invited Jason for dinner, and told him that he was welcome any time. They were very warm and friendly; at first Jason thought this was because he had saved their little girl. The family was grateful, extremely so, but...

He started to visit from time to time, and he saw the same warm welcome extend to anybody who came in. The family was warm, and emotional, and playful, and as time passed, Jason began to know the specific people —

Emma, the matron who had first invited in, was wise, gentle, and motherly. She was a big woman with an even bigger heart, that seemed to have ample room for anybody who came into the house. She was the person most in charge.

Harold, her younger brother, was full of stories and jokes. He was the life of gatherings, and often had people laughing. He was the person who had travelled the most throughout the United States, and seemed to have his finger on the pulse of the nation — how it had changed, how it had stayed the same, throughout the years.

Jane was Edna's eldest daughter, and the mother of the little girl whom Jason saved. All of the people in the family had an easy-going, warm, welcoming manner — it really was not long before Jason felt as if he were one of the family — but the welcome seemed to crystallize in Jane. She took the most effort to include Jason, and asked him the most questions.

Alfred was Jane's husband. He worked at a factory, and was quite the musician; he played several instruments, and often managed to get the whole family singing and dancing.

Anne was Edna's second daughter, and was perhaps most actively involved in race relations and the womanist movement. Through him, Jason saw a kind of feminism which was completely different; what most struck Jason was that, in its adamant advocacy of womanhood and motherhood, neither Anne nor any of her other womanist friends found any need for abortion, or regarded children as an inconvenience.

Erica, the little girl whom Jason saved, was a little ball of life. She was insatiably curious and inquisitive; more than once, she managed to put Jason somewhat on the spot: "Why you a comin' heah? Da other white folk doan come heah much, like they afraid of us, o' sumthin'." — but she asked in perfect innocence and sincerity, and the open warmth of the others (especially Jane) defused the tension. She was also quite a cuddlebug, and (Jason eventually discovered) more than a little bit ticklish.

Steve, Alfred and Edna's second child, wanted to be a scientist; he was somewhat quiet, and a bookworm. Jason was sometimes amazed by his intelligence, and was able to talk with him about some of the things he had learned from Senex.

Ronald, the baby of Alfred and Edna's family, was full of energy, and energy, and energy, and energy. He would run around the house all day long, and it did not take long for Jason to learn what was Ron's favorite word: "Again!" He seemed to have a tireless enjoyment of the things he knew.

Monica had been adopted by the family, and (in a sense) was Anne's baby. The two of them were quite close, and she seemed to be able to learn very quickly anything

Anne told her.

There were also a number of neighborhood children going in and out of the house; the family treasured them, and seemed to welcome them as if they were their own. James wanted to be a pilot; Michael was very much interested in fire, and loved the Fourth of July; Desiree loved to dance with anyone and everyone; Edward chased the other children around.

Jason cherished his moments visiting the apartment, and grew especially fond of Erica. She would often sit on his lap and try to understand the things Jason was talking about (though Jason tended to too often talk about things that were rather complex to reasonably expect a child to understand), and would often playfully tell him how funny he was. Jason came to love the music, the dancing, the laughter, the emotion. He was struck by how different the family was — and how human.

As he came out of the apartment, he saw Senex walking towards him, and tipping his hat. "I am pleased," Senex said, "and I think that you are ready to enter."

XIII

Senex said, "Are you ready to hear a story?"

Jason said, "I think I am."

Senex said, "This is the most important story that I will ever tell you."

Jason said, "I am listening."

Senex began, "Once upon a time, there was a coruscating Light, a surge of power, a rock greater than a mountain. And from this Light was begotten... another facet of the same eternal Eternal essence. Father and Son. Between them shot a fire of love and energy. In and among and from them were glory, majesty, light, power, love, goodness.

"And the Light spoke, and star upon star upon star upon star poured fourth, pulsing with life. They all joined in the great Dance, and spun and turned in wheel within wheel within wheel within wheel. As they danced the great Dance and sung the great Song, the Light and all of the stars revelled in the glory and beauty.

"The first and most glorious of the stars that were formed, held a place in the dance that was second only to the Light itself. The very least of the stars held a place of glory to contemplate for a lifetime, and this was the greatest.

"Then the first star turned, and stepped out of the harmony of the dance, and spoke to the Light. He demanded to be placed above the Light, to lead the Dance himself. 'I am the greatest of the stars; I am greater and wiser and more glorious than you. Cede to me my rightful place.'"

There was something about the demand that jarred Jason, filling him with revulsion to the very core. In it, he saw the essence of everything that is perverse and vile and impure. He wondered why the Light did not blast the star out of existence right there.

"The Light paused, and then said, 'You believe that you are better than me.

"'You believe that you are wiser than me.

"'Prove it.

"'You and your glory were the beginning of my plan; you are not the end of it. I have a plan deep within my heart. You may form whatever plan your wisdom may find for you. And we will let the plans play out, and we will see whose plan is the wiser - yours or mine.'

"And then the star screamed out his blasphemous accord, screamed a scream that tore the very fabric of space. And a third of the stars joined him in his rebellion, and became dragons, and serpents, and worms.

"Thus began a cosmic war.

"The Light again created, a creation that was vivid and new and detailed and wondrous. Slowly, with the patience of an artist, he formed rocks, mountains, and trees. The smallest blade of grass was perfect. He formed a great rock surrounded by lights, then plants which live, then animals which move, then finally men in his own image, likeness, and glory. When he stopped to rest, all of the stars stood watching in awe.

"Then the darkened star came, in the form of a serpent, and beguiled man, to do the one thing that is accursed. And the man and woman, created as immortal gods, bore in them a curse, and began to die from the inside out. They, also, stepped out of the harmony of the dance and out of the source of health; their spirits rotted in vice and evil, and the worm began to infest and grow inside their hearts. There was perversity after perversity after perversity after perversity. One generation after the first sin, came the first murder: brother murdered brother. And the people were quick to embrace evil and forget what is good, even the Light himself.

"And all of the dragons, and serpents, and worms, cackled and screeched with unholy laughter, and the stars winced in pain. The first of Dragons taunted the Light: 'Your plan? Your glorious and wise plan? You have indeed made a fine creation for me to soil. Thank you; I very much enjoy watching the curses grow and multiply.'

"And the men grow wicked, so that they all deserved to die.

"All but one.

"One man walked in the Light.

"And the Light called out to the one man. 'You. You there in the desert, where neither rain nor mist dampen the earth.'

"And the man answered, 'Yes?'

"And the Light commanded, 'Build an immense boat.'

"And the dragons and worms cackled and jeered.

"And the man, ridiculed and cursed by even his friends, built an immense boat.

"And the great Dragon said, 'One candle? You hope by lighting one single candle to vanquish a whole world of darkness? Come, old fool; it doesn't work that way.'

"And the Light remained silent.

"Then the Light called to a man, and told him, 'Leave your kin, your land, your family, everything that is dear to you, and I will give you a son, and make you into a great nation.'

"And the man took up his belongings and left.

"And the Light gave the man a son, and the son grew and matured.

"Then the Light told the man, 'Take your son, whom you love, and sacrifice him to me.'

"And the man obeyed, taking the son up on the mountain to sacrifice. He raises his arm, knife in hand, to strike the child dead.

"And the Light, quick as lightning, sent a star to say, 'Stop. Because you have not withheld from me even your son, I will bless you richly.'

"And the Dragon says, 'What's the point of this? Do you call one or two righteous men to help us see how evil all the rest are? Or could it just be that you are unwilling to admit defeat?'

"And the Light remained silent.

"And in the great Dragon, was the faintest tremor of fear.

"Then the Light called another man, and told him to forsake riches and luxury to free his people from slavery. The man hesitated, shied away from the task before him - and ultimately obeyed.

"Then the great dragon said, 'Can't you just end it now? I know that you've lost, but I'm beginning to feel uncomfortable.'

"And the Light continues his work.

"Through the man, the Light gave a law, showing what is right and what is wrong. And the people - staggeringly, and with many misgivings - started to obey.

"Then the Dragon came to the Light, and the Light said of another man, 'Have you seen this servant of mine? He is upright and blameless.'

"The Dragon scoffed and said, 'Well, of course! Look at all the prosperity you have given him. That is why he worships you. Take it away, and he will curse you to your face.'

"The Light said, 'Prove it. I give you permission to take away everything that he holds dear to him - only do not touch his body.'

"The Dragon breathed fire, and destroys the man's livestock, his possessions, his children. And the man wept in misery. He was told to curse the Light and die. In agony, he screamed in pain and cursed even the day of his birth - but refuses to curse the Light.

"Then the Dragon said, "You know, a man will give everything he owns for his health. You have given this man abundant health - and he is still healthy. Only take that away, and he will curse you to your face.'

"And again, the Light gave permission, only requiring that the dragon not slay him. And the man was covered in painful sores from head to toe, his body wracked with pain, tortured. He was in agony. When three of his friends came, they sat with him for a week in silence because his pain is so great. And still, the man refused to curse the Light.

"The friends then talked, insisting that the man had done wrong, yet he does not even accept their claim. Finally the Light came and spoke through a storm, healing the man and restoring what was lost twice over.

"And the stars rejoiced.

"Then the Light pulled another corner of the veil off of his plan. The Light begotten was sent, and became a man himself, suffering and walking the dust of the fallen world. He called people, telling them to abandon net and boat to follow him - and they obeyed. He healed the sick, diseased, and injured; he casts out fallen stars who have taken possession of people. The dragon attacked again again, trying to have him killed, and tempting him in every way. And yet the Light in earth remained pure and blameless. He began to call people about him, and teach them.

"Then one of the Light's closest friends betrayed him, and the Light himself was hung out and exposed to die. And when the Light died, darkness reigned.

"And the dragons, and serpents, and worms, jeered and cackled. And the great Dragon taunts, 'Your great and wise plan gave me an even greater victory than I had hoped for. I set about to destroy your creation - and now I have destroyed your uncreated Son.'

"And tears flowed.

"Then a surge of light and power flowed, and the begotten Light was alive, transformed, coursing with the power of an indestructible life, and bearing with him the cure for the curse. And the fire of love and energy flowing among and in and from the Light flowed into his followers, too. The Light ascends back into Heaven from whence he came - and dwelt inside them.

"And in the community of those who believe and accept his cure, heroes and martyrs stand for the truth and fought, alongside the stars, against the darkness. And as all were watching — the Light, the stars, and also the dead, that is those who walked before, and now stood cheering those who walk now as they continue in the battle — the wisdom of the plan formed by the Light was revealed in the community of those who believe. In this community, in those whom the Light again draws into the great Dance, was

"A large family of many children for the Light
Mother, and brother, and sister for the begotten Light
A body for the begotten Light to live in
A dwelling place and temple for the eternal fire of love and energy
A witness to the world
A moral preserver and purifier to the world
A servant to the world
A warrior against the great Dragon

"With all of its faults and foibles, the community reached out, and invited others also to step into the Dance.

"Then, as the begotten Light left the world, he returned - in full, unveiled glory and majesty, with all of the stars with him. The dead and the living members of the community were imbued with the same life as he has, their bodies transformed, and shared in the divine nature. The earth was destroyed in a great apocalypse, then remade even better than before. All — the living and the dead alike — were brought forth, and brought to account for their life and deeds; those who had chosen a curse were accursed, and those who had chosen were imbued with life beyond intense. And it was before the renewed, regenerated, transformed community of believers that the Dragon stood, and saw the wisdom of the plan. And it was below their feet that the Light crushed the Dragon, before casting it and all of its minions into a lake of fire. And all of those watching saw in full, not only that the Light is more powerful, but also the immeasurably greater wisdom."

After a time, Jason said, "That is the most beautiful story I have ever heard."

Senex said, "Would you like to have slain the worm that is inside your heart? Would you like to dance the great Dance?"

Jason said, "Yes, I would."

Senex said, "The story is true, and we are now living between the first and second comings of the Light. And he bears with him the cure for the curse — and, if you ask him, he will help you slay the worm that is inside your heart, and let you join his forces to fight the darkness that is in the world."

"How do I do that?"

Senex said, "You must pray a prayer, something like,

"'Lord Jesus, come into my heart.
Forgive my sins.
Draw me into your Light.

Fill me with your Life.
Make me your own.
I give myself to you,
And accept you giving yourself to me.'"

A look of surprise crossed Jason's face. "Is this Christianity?"

"Yes."

Jason's surprise turned to disgust. "But Christianity is narrow-minded and intolerant and repressive and archaic and — You deceived me, and tricked me into thinking it was something beautiful!"

"Jason, have you ever heard Plato's allegory of the cave?"

"No."

"Plato made an allegory, which was more or less as follows:

"Imagine that there is a cave. In this cave are prisoners who have been there from birth. They are shackled, and held in place.

"Behind the prisoners is a wall, and behind the wall a fire.

"People carry things back and forth, above the wall, so that they cast great, flickering shadows on the wall. And as these prisoners grow up, they will never see what a chair, or a book, or a sword looks like. They will only see the shadows on the wall.

"And they will become very good at identifying and recognizing the shadows, and think that they are the realities themselves. They won't think that a pot is a pot. They will think that the shadow is a pot.

"Now imagine that one of these prisoners is brought out of the cave, into the world. He will first be blinded by the light, and then only slowly be able to see. He will see nothing he will recognize, and he will curse those who brought him out.

"But, eventually, he will learn to see — and he will see

things infinitely fuller, and richer, and more real than ever before. He will see the realities that cast the shadows.

"Now imagine that he is taken back in the cave again. At first, he won't be able to see anything in the darkness; the others in the cave will believe that he is blind. When he does adjust, he will begin to speak of realities beyond the shadows, which are far greater than what is seen — and the other people will think him mad as well as blind. They will vow to kill anyone who should take anyone else up out of what they believe is reality, into the light."

Senex paused a moment, and then continued.

"There are two things which I would like to say.

"The first is that there are a lot of evil Christians, and Christians have done a lot of bad things. I have been bored by a lot of dull Christians, and hurt by a lot of hypocritical Christians. And I am ashamed of a great deal of what has been done in the name of Christ."

"The second is that what you have seen called 'Christianity' is only a shadow cast in bad light. What I have been doing is helping you to see the reality itself, in the light of the sun."

"But why didn't you tell me it was Christianity to begin with? Wasn't that deceptive?"

"I did not tell you for a reason. I wanted to un-deceive you, and show you the reality itself. If I told you that I wanted to show you Christianity, you would have thought I meant the ugly shadow that is called Christianity — and would you have wanted to know anything about it?"

Jason begrudgingly said, "No."

After a time, Senex said, "I can see by your face that you have more questions. What are they?"

"They are questions you won't like."

"Ask them."

"What about the Inquisition? What about the intolerance? What about saying that all those other people's religions are wrong? What about saying that everyone else is damned to Hell?"

"The Inquisition was one of the darkest moments in Christian history, and it has done damage that hurts people down to this day. It, along with the Crusades has fractured the relationships Christians have with Muslims and Jews to this day. And it does another, even deeper damage. It makes people believe that standing for the truth is evil."

"But what about not accepting other religions? What about Hell?"

"Jason, do you know the worm inside your heart?"

"Yes."

"The worm is inside my heart, too. It is in everybody's heart. And it needs to be killed again and again and again. And, if you do not fight it to the death, it will kill you."

"But... I still don't see why you have to be so intolerant."

"Jason, if I am shot in the arm, can a doctor help me?"

"Yes. He can help stitch you up, so your body can heal."

"What if I refuse to be stitched up? What if I shoot myself again and again, and insist that the doctor heal me without stitching me up or stopping me from shooting myself?"

"But... the doctor can't help you because you won't let him."

"That's right, Jason. A doctor can't help you if you choose injury over medicine. And Jesus is a doctor with the only medicine that works.

"I don't believe in Hell because I want to think about people dying. I believe in Hell for the same reason I believe that shooting yourself is bad for your health — because that's the way it is. I know that other religions are things people put a lot of work into, and take very seriously. But they are not the doctor's medicine, and the cold, harsh reality is that taking the medicine — all of it — is the only way to be healed."

"What about homosexuals? Can't they be Christians like everyone else?"

"Homosexuals can be Christians just like everyone else, the exact same way that everyone else is a Christian.

Namely, by letting the doctor heal all of their injuries. All of us have different wounds, and they all need to be healed. I have wounds that most homosexuals don't. I am a recovering alcoholic. I haven't had a drink for sixteen years now, but I spent twenty years of my life as a drunkard. Whatever wounds we have, be they homosexual lust, or drinking too much alcohol, or pride, or any of ten thousand other sins, we need to have them to be healed. All of them."

Jason thought for a while, and then said, "This is the most difficult thing that anyone has ever asked me. I don't know if I can do it."

Senex said, "I know it's difficult, and I can't do it by myself. But there is help. It is a difficult path, but the Light will give you the strength, and give me the strength. And remember the community in the story? They will help you, as they help me."

Jason leaned back, and thought for a time. Then he closed his eyes, trembled, and prayed,

> "Lord Jesus, come into my heart.
> Forgive my sins.
> Draw me into your Light.
> Fill me with your Life.
> Make me your own.
> I give myself to you,
> And accept you giving yourself to me."

And angels rejoiced.
And Jason entered another world.

The Wagon, the Blackbird, and the Saab

Before I get further, I'd like to say a few words about what I drive.

I drive an Oldsmobile F-85 station wagon. What's the color? When people are being nice, they talk about a classic, subdued camouflage color. Sometimes the more candid remarks end up saying something like, "The Seventies called. They want their paint job back," although my station wagon is a 1965 model. All in all, I think I had the worst car of anyone I knew. Or at least that's what I *used* to think.

Then I changed my mind. Or maybe it would be better to say that I had my mind changed for me.

I was sitting at the cafeteria, when I saw someone looking for a place to sit. He was new, and I motioned for him to come over. He sat down, quietly, and ate in silence. There was a pretty loud conversation at the table, and when people started talking about cars, his eyes seemed to widen. I asked him what kind of car he drove.

After hesitating, he mumbled something hard to understand, and looked like he was getting smaller. Someone said, "Maybe he doesn't drive a car at all," and whatever he mumbled was forgotten in raucous laughter.

I caught him in the hallway later, and he asked if I could

help him move several large boxes that were not in the city. When we made the trip, he again seemed to be looking around with round eyes, almost enchanted by my rustbucket.

I began to feel sorry for the chap, and I gave him rides. Even if I didn't understand.

He still managed to dodge any concrete hint of whatever it was that got him around—and I had a hunch that he hadn't just walked. My other friends may have given me some ribbing about my bucket of bolts, but really it was just ribbing. I tried to impress on him that he would be welcome even if he just got around on a derelict moped— but still not a single peep.

By the time it was becoming old to joke about whatever he drove, I accepted a dare and shadowed him as he walked along a couple of abandoned streets, got to the nearest airstrip...

and got into an SR-71 Blackbird. The man took off in an SR-71 Blackbird. *An SR-71 Blackbird!* Words failed me. Polite ones, at any rate. The SR-71 Blackbird may be the coolest looking reconnaissance plane ever; as far as looks go, it beats the pants off the spacecraft in a few science fiction movies. But the engineers weren't really trying to look cool; that was a side effect of trying to make an aircraft that *was* cool. It has those sleek lines because it's a bit of a stealth aircraft; it *can* be detected by radar, but it's somewhat harder. And suppose you're in an SR-71 Blackbird and you *are* picked up by radar, and enemy soldiers launch a surface-to-air missle at you—or two, or ten? Just speed up and you'll outrun it; the SR-71 Blackbird is the fastest aircraft ever built. Some SR-71 Blackbirds have been shot *at*. Ain't never got one shot *down*. One of the better surface-to-air rockets has about the same odds of hitting an SR-71 Blackbird doing Mach 3.2 as a turtle trying to catch up with a cheetah and *ram* it. An SR-71 Blackbird is a different kind of rare. It's not just that it's not a common electronic device that you can pick up at any decent

department store; it isn't even like something very
expensive and rare that has a waiting list is almost never on
store shelves. The SR-71 Blackbird is more like, if anything,
an invention that the inventor can't sell—perhaps, some
years back, one of the first, handmade electric light bulbs—
because it is so far from how people think and do things
that they can't see anyone would *want* to use them. The SR-
71 Blackbird is rare enough that few pilots have even seen it.
And I saw, or thought I saw, my friend get into one.

and got into an SR-71 Blackbird. The man took off in an
SR-71 Blackbird. *An SR-71 Blackbird!* Words failed me.
Polite ones, at any rate. And probably the impolite ones,
too. The SR-71 Blackbird may be the coolest looking
reconnaissance plane ever; as far as looks go, it beats the
pants off the spacecraft in a few science fiction movies. But
the engineers weren't really trying to look cool; that was a
side effect of trying to make an aircraft that *was* cool. It has
those sleek lines because it's a bit of a stealth aircraft; it *can*
be detected by radar, but it's somewhat harder. And
suppose you're in an SR-71 Blackbird and you *are* picked up
by radar, and enemy soldiers launch a surface-to-air missle
at you—or two, or ten? Just speed up and you'll outrun it;
the SR-71 Blackbird is the fastest aircraft ever built. Some
SR-71 Blackbirds have been shot *at*. Ain't never got one shot
down. One of the better surface-to-air rockets has about the
same odds of hitting an SR-71 Blackbird doing Mach 3.2 as
a turtle trying to catch up with a cheetah and *ram* it. An SR-
71 Blackbird is a different kind of rare. It's not just that it's
not a common electronic device that you can pick up at any
decent department store; it isn't even like something very
expensive and rare that has a waiting list is almost never on
store shelves. The SR-71 Blackbird is more like, if anything,
an invention that the inventor can't sell—perhaps, some
years back, one of the first, handmade electric light bulbs—
because it is so far from how people think and do things
that they can't see anyone would *want* to use them. The SR-
71 Blackbird is rare enough that few pilots have even seen it.

And I saw, or thought I saw, my friend get into one.

I walked back in a daze, sat down, decided not to take any drinks just then, and cornered the joker, who couldn't keep his mouth shut. I told him to fess up about whatever he slipped me, but he was clueless—and when I couldn't keep my mouth shut and blabbed why, he didn't believe me. (Not that I blame him; I didn't believe it myself.)

I ate by myself, later, and followed him. The third time, I caught him in the act.

I was red with anger, and almost saw red.

He blanched whiter than at the wisecrack about him maybe not driving a car.

What I would have said then, if I were calmer, was, "Do you think it's right for a billionaire, to go around begging? You have things that none of us even dream of, and you—?"

After I had yelled at him, he looked at me and said, "How can I fuel up?"

I glared at him. "I don't know, but it's got to be much cooler than waiting in line at a gas station."

"Maybe it is cooler, but I don't think so, and that's not what I asked. Suppose I want to fly in my airplane. What do I do to be fueled up?"

"Um, a fuel truck drives out and fills you up?"

"And then I'm good to go because I have a full tank, just like you?"

"I don't see what you're getting at."

"Ok, let me ask you. What do you do if you want to make a long trip? Can you fill your tank, maybe a day or two before your trip, and leave?"

"Yes. And that would be true if you had a moped, or a motorcycle, or a luxury car, or even something exotic like an ATV or a hovercraft."

"But not an SR-71 Blackbird."

"What do you mean, not an SR-71 Blackbird? Did you get a good deal because your aircraft is broken?"

"Um, just because you can assume something in a good car, or even a bad car, doesn't mean that it's true across the board. When it's sitting on the ground, my aircraft leaks fuel."

"It leaks fuel? Why are you flying an aircraft that's not broken?"

"There's a difference between designing a passenger car and what I deal with. With a passenger car, if the manufacturers are any good, the car can sit with little to no fuel leak even if it's badly maintained."

"But this does not apply to what the rest of us can only dream of?"

"No."

"Why not?"

"A passenger car heats up a little, at top speeds, due to air friction. One and the same part works for the fuel line when it's been in the garage for an hour, and when it's driving as fast as you've driven it. Not so with my aircraft. The SR-71 Blackbird is exposed to one set of temperatures in the hangar, and then there is air friction for moving at Mach 3.2, and there's a basic principle of physics that says that what gets hotter, gets bigger."

"What's your point?"

"The parts that make up an SR-71 Blackbird are one size in the hangar and other sizes when the aircraft is flying at high speeds. The engineers could have sized the parts so that you could keep an aircraft in the hangar without losing any fuel... or they could make an airplane that leaks fuel on the ground, but it works when it was flying. But they could not make an airplane that would work at Mach 3.2 *and* have a sealed fuel line in the hangar... and that means that, when I go anywhere worth mentioning in my hot, exciting airplane, even I get fueled up on the ground, and I lose quite a lot of fuel getting airborne and more or less need an immediate air-to-air refueling... This is besides the obvious fact that I can't run on *any* fuel an ordinary gas station would carry. For that matter, the JP-7, a strange beast of a 'fuel' that must also serve as hydraulic fluid and *engine coolant*, is about as exotic compared to most jet fuel as it is compared to the 'boring' gasoline which you take for granted—you can't get fuel for an SR-71 Blackbird at a regular airport any more than you can buy 'ordinary' jet fuel at a regular gas station... and you think me strange when I get excited about the fact that you can drive up to any normal gas station and fill-er-up!"

I hesitated, and then asked, "But besides one or two details like—"

He cut me off. "It's not 'one or two details,' any more than—than filling out paperwork and dealing with bureaucracy amounts to 'one or two details' of a police officer's life. Sure, on television, something exciting happens to police officers every hour, but a real police officer's life is *extremely* different from police shows. It's not just paperwork. Perhaps there is *lots* of paperwork—a police officer deals with at least as much paperwork and bureaucracy as an employee who's a cog in a big office—but there are other things. Police officers get in firefights all the time on TV. But this is another area where TV's image is not the reality. I've known police officers who wouldn't trade their work for anything in the world. Doesn't mean that their work is like a cop show. When police officers aren't being filmed on those videos that make dramatic shows, and they aren't training, the average police officer starts firing maybe once every three or four years. There are many, many seasoned veterans who have never fired a gun on the street. And having an SR-71 Blackbird is no more what you'd imagine it was like to have a cool, neat, super-duper reconnaissance plane instead of your unsatisfying, meagre, second-rate, dull car than... than... than being a police officer has all the excitement of surviving a shootout every day, but only having to fill paperwork once every three or four years if at all!"

"Um, what else is there?"

"Um, what's a typical trip for you? I mean, with your car?"

"My wife's family is at the other side of the state, and—"

"So that's an example of a common trip? More common than shopping or driving to meet someone?"

"Ok; often I'm just running some errands."

"Such a boring thing to do with a station wagon. If you want things to get interesting, try something I wouldn't brave."

"What?"

"Go for the gusto. Borrow *my* vehicle! First, you can fuel up at home, as any fuel that had been in your tank is now a slippery puddle underneath the vehicle you wish you had. Then start the vehicle. You'll have something to deal with later, after the hot exhaust sets your trees on fire. And maybe a building or two. Then lurch around, and try to taxi along the streets. (Let's assume you don't set any trees on fire, which is not likely.) Now you're used to be able to see most of the things on the road, at least the ones you don't want to hit? And—"

"Ok, *ok*, I get the idea! The SR-71 Blackbird is the worst, most pitiable—"

"Perhaps I have misspoken. Or at least wasn't clear enough. I wasn't trying to say that it's simple torture flying an SR-71 Blackbird. There are few things as joyful as flying. And do you know what kind of possibilities exist (in everything from friendship to work to hobbies) when the list of things you can easily make a day trip to the other side of the globe? When—"

"Then why the big deal you just made before?"

"An SR-71 Blackbird is many things, but it is not what you imagine if you fantasize about everything you imagine my vehicle to be, *and assume almost everything you take for granted in yours*. There are a great many nice things that go without saying in your vehicle, that aren't part of mine. You know, a boring old station wagon with its dull room for a driver plus a few passengers and some cargo, that runs on the most mundane petroleum-based fuel you can get, and of course is familiar to most mechanics and can be maintained by almost any real automotive shop, and—if this is even worth mentioning—can be driven safely across a major network of roads, and—*of course* this can be taken for granted in any real vehicle—has a frame that gives you a fighting chance of surviving a full-speed collision with—"

"Ok, *ok*, I get the picture. But wouldn't it have helped matters if you would tell people these things up front? You know, maybe something about avoiding these confrontations, or maybe something about 'Honesty is the best policy'?"

He said, "Ok. So when I meet people, I should say, 'Hi. My vehicle leaves Formula One racecars in the dust. It also flies, can slip through radar, and does several things you can't even imagine. But don't worry, I haven't let any of this go to my head. I'm not full of myself. I promise I won't look down on you or whatever car you drive. And you can promise not to feel the least bit envious, inferior, or intimated. *Deal*?' It seems to come across that way no matter *how* I try to make that point. And really, why shouldn't it?"

I paused. "Do our vehicles have *anything* in common at all?"

"Yes—more than either of us can understand."

"But what on earth, if we're so different? My vehicle is a 1965 model; your vehicle sounds so new you'd need a time machine to get one—"

"My vehicle is a 1965 model too."

"If you want to lie and make me feel better, you could have told me that your vehicle was years older than mine."

"I meant it. There is something about our vehicles that is cut from the same cloth."

"How can you say that? I mean, without stretching? Is what they have in common that they're both in the same universe? Or that they're both bigger than an atom but smaller than a galaxy? Or some other way of *really* stretching?"

"If you want to dig deeper, have you read, 'I, Pencil'? Where an economist speaks on behalf of a common, humble pencil?"

"A speech from a pencil? What does that have to do with our vehicles? Are you going to compare our vehicles to a pencil?"

"Yes."

"So you're stretching."

"No."

"In I, Pencil, a cheap wooden pencil explains what it took to make it. It talks about how a diamond in the rough— I mean, graphite in the rough—crosses land and sea and is combined with clay, and a bit of this and that to make the exquisite slender shaft we call pencil 'lead'. The wood comes from the majestic cedar—do you know what it takes to make a successful logging operation—and then a mind-boggling number of steps transform a hundred feet of tree into something that's a little hard to explain, but machined to very precise specifications, and snapped together before six coats of laquer—oh, I forgot, before the cedar wraps around the slender graphite wand, it's also adorned by being tinted a darker color, 'for the same reason women put rouge on their faces' or something like that. Its parts come through a transportation network from all over the world, and the rubber eraser—which wouldn't erase at all well if were just rubber; it needs to be a cocktail of ingredients that perform at least three major tasks if it will work as an eraser. Try erasing pencil with a rubber ball sometime; it will erase terribly if it erases at all. Your erases is not mere rubber, but a rubber alloy, the way airplanes are made, not with mere aluminum, but with an aluminum alloy, and—"

"So the parts of a pencil have an interesting story?"

"Yes. And the quite impressive way they are put together—pencils don't assemble themselves, and a good machine—for some steps—costs a king's ransom. And the way they're distributed, and any number of things necessary for business to run the whole process, and—"

"Then should I start offering my daughter's pencils to a museum?"

"I wouldn't *exactly* offer one of her pencils to a museum. Museums do not have room for every wonder this world has. But I will say this. The next pencil you forget somewhere wouldn't have been yours to lose without more work, talent, skill, knowledge, venture capital, and a thousand other things than it took to make a wonder like the Rosetta Stone or the Mona Lisa."

As usual, she was dressed to kill. Her outfit was modest —I can almost say, *ostentatiously modest*—but, somehow, demurely made the point that she might be a model.

I had a bad feeling about something. During our conversation on the way over, I said, "You have an issue with Saab drivers." He replied, "No. Or yes, but it's beside the point. Saab drivers tend to have issues with me." I was caught off-guard: "That sounds as arrogant as anything I've —"

He asked me to forget what he had said. For the rest of the conversation, he seemed to be trying to change the subject.

She greeted us, shook his hand warmly, and turned back. "—absolutely brilliant. Not, in any way, like the British Comet, which never should have been flown in the first place, and was part of why jumbo jetliners were dangerous in the public's eye. The training for people who were going to be in that jumbo jetliner—the Comet—included being in a vacuum so that soldiers would know what to do if they were flying in a sparse layer of the atmosphere and the airplane simply disintegrated around them and left them in what might as well have been a vacuum. This sort of thing *happened* with enough jumbo jetliners that the public was very leery of them. For good reason, they were considered a disaster looking for a place to happen.

"And so, when Boeing effectively bet the company on the Boeing 707—like they did with every new airplane; it wasn't just one product among others that could be a flop without killing the company—they gave the test pilot very careful instructions about what to do when he demonstrated their new jumbo jetliner.

"At the airshow, he was flying along, and after a little while, people began to notice that one of the airplane's wings was lower, and the other was higher...

"The Boeing 707 test pilot was doing a barrel roll, which is extremely rough on an airplane. It's like... something like, instead of saying that a computer is tough, throwing it across the room. This stunt was a surprise to the other people at Boeing, almost as much as to the other, and it wasn't long before Boeing got on the radio and asked the pilot, 'What the §±¤¶ do you think you're doing?' The pilot's reply was short, and to the point:

"'Why, selling airplanes, sir.'

"He told a reporter afterwards, 'And when I got done with that barrel roll, I realized that the people weren't going to *believe* what they just saw... so I turned around and I did another one!'"

A moment later, someone else said, "What does 'Saab' mean again? You've told me, but—"

She smiled. "It took me a while to remember, too. 'SAAB' stands for '*Svenska aeroplan Aktiebolaget*,' literally 'Swedish Aeroplane Limited.' It's a European aerospace company that decided that besides making fighter jets and military aircraft, they would run a side business of selling cars, or at least the kind of car you get when you combine a muscle car, a luxury vehicle, and more than a touch of a military jet. It's like an airplane in big and small ways— everything from, if you unbuckle your seatbelt, a 'Fasten seatbelts' light just like an airliners', to the rush of power you feel when you hit the gas and might as well be lifting off... I'm not sure how you would describe it... It's almost what Lockheed-Martin would sell if they were Scandinavian and wanted to sell something you could drive on the street."

He said, "It sounds like a delight to drive."

She said, "It is. Would you two like me to take you out for a spin? I'd be delighted to show it to you. What kind of car do you drive?"

He paused for a split second and said, "I needed to get a ride with him; I have nothing that I could use to get over here."

I told her, "He's being modest."

She looked at me quizzically. "How?"

"He flies an SR-71 Blackbird... um... sorry, I shouldn't have said that just as you were taking a drink."

He seemed suddenly silent. For that matter, the room suddenly seemed a whole lot quieter.

She said, "You're joking, right?"

No one said a word.

Then she said, "Wow. It is a privilege and an honor. I have never met someone who..."

He said, "I really don't understand... maybe... um... I'm not really *better*, or—"

She said, "Stop being modest. I'd love to hear more about your fighter. Have you shot anything down?"

He looked as if he was thinking very hurriedly, and not finding the thought that he wanted.

"The SR-71 Blackbird would be pretty useless in a dogfight. It is neither designed or equipped to fight even with a very obsolete enemy aircraft; it's just designed to snoop around and gather information."

She said, "Um, so they get shot down all the time? Wouldn't you tend to get a lot of missiles fired by enemy fighters who aren't worried about you shooting back? What do you do when you run out of countermeasure flares?"

He paused for a moment, saying, "The SR-71 Blackbird doesn't have anything you'd expect. Flares are a great way to decoy a heat-seeking missile, but the SR-71 Blackbird doesn't have them, either."

I turned to him and said, "You're being almost disturbingly modest." Then I turned to her and said, "An SR-71 Blackbird can go over three times the speed of sound.

The standard evasive to a surface-to-air rocket is simply to accelerate until you've left the rocket in the dust. I'm not aware of one of them being shot down."

Her eyes were as big as dinner plates.

She said, "I am stunned. I have talked with a few pilots, but I have never met anyone close to an SR-71 Blackbird pilot. I hope we can be friends." She stood close to him and offered her hand.

The three of us ran into each other a number of times in the following days. She seemed to want to know everything about his aircraft, and seemed very respectful, or at least seemed to be working hard to convey how impressed she was.

It was a dark and stormy night. He and I were both on our way out the door, when she asked, "What are you doing?"

He said, "I want to try some challenges. I plan on going out over the ocean and manoeuvering in the storm system."

She turned to him and said, very slowly, "No, you're not."

He turned to me and said, "C'mon, let's go."

She said, "Are you crazy? A storm like that has done what enemy rockets have failed to do: take down your kind of craft. I've grown quite fond of you, and I'd hate to see you get killed because you were being stupid. Think about 61-7969 / 2020."

He said, "May I ask why you know about that?"

"I have been doing some reading because I want to understand you. And I understand people well enough, and care about you enough, to tell when you are acting against your best interests."

He grabbed my arm and forced me out the door. Once in the car, he said, "I'm sorry... I needed to get out before saying something I would regret."

"Like what?"

"'So you know just the perfect way to straighten me out, and you don't even need to ask me questions. Walk a mile in my shoes, to a place you can reach in a car but not my aircraft, and then we might be able to talk.'"

I watched him take off, and I came back to pick him up, after waiting an hour. I could tell something that seemed not quite perfect about his flying, but I do not regret that I kept my mouth shut about that.

The next day she surprised us by meeting us first thing in the morning.

She gave us a stack of paper. "I care about you quite a lot, and I don't want to be invited to your funeral in the next year. Here are detailed aviation regulations and international laws which are intended for your safety. I could not get an exact count of the number of crimes you committed, either for last night or for your reckless day-to-day flying around. I am sure that there are many responsible ways a vehicle like yours can be used, and I have inquired about whether there are any people who can offer some guidance and free you to..."

He turned around, took my elbow, and began walking out to the parking lot. We got in my car, and she raced for hers.

I saw her go to the mouth of the parking lot and then stop. The one Rolls-Royce in town had broken down, of all places *there*, and the owner and chauffer were both outside. I had thought that the person who was chauffered in a Rolls-Royce was a peaceful sort of man, but he was yelling then, and before she got over the owner positively erupted at the chauffeur and waved his arms. She had gotten out and wanted to talk with them, but you can't get a word in edgewise at a time like that.

Now I'd like to clarify something about my car. I've only seen a vehicle like mine in a demolition derby once, but I was surprised. I wasn't surprised, in particular, that the wagon was the last vehicle moving. What I was surprised at was that over a third of the derby had passed before the ugly wagon started to crumple at all.

And one other thing: one April Fools' Day, a friend who drives a sleek, sporty little 1989 Chrysler LeBaron gave me a bumper sticker that said, "Zero to sixty in fifteen minutes," and then acted surprised when I challenged him to a short race. When the race had finished, he seemed extraordinarily surprised, and I told him, "There is a question on your face. Let me answer it." Then I opened the hood on my ugly, uncool station wagon and said, "Your sleek little number can get by on a 2.2 liter engine. Do you know what *that* is?" He said, "Um, the engine?" And I said, "That is a 6.6 liter V8. Any questions?"

Ok, enough clarification. I looked around, turned in the opposite direction, and floored my car, blasting through the hedges and getting heavy scrapes on the bottom of my car. I got shortly on the road, and had a straight shot at the airport. She did eventually catch up to me, but not until there was nothing left to see but some hot exhaust and the fuel that had leaked when he tried to take off. (I still get the occasional note from him.)

Besides worrying about him, I was also much less worried about my car: tough as it is, cars don't like getting their undersides scraped on gravel, and I decided to take my car to the garage and have the mechanic take a look at it and tell me if I broke anything.

I was surprised—though maybe I shouldn't have been— to see the Rolls-Royce in the garage when I pulled in. I intended to explain that I might have scraped the bottom up, and after I did so, my curiosity got the better of me. I asked something about Rolls-Royces breaking down.

The mechanic gave me the oddest look.

I asked him, "Why the funny look?"

He opened the hood, and said, "Rolls-Royces do break down easily... and it's even easier to break down if you open the hood, jam a screwdriver right *there*, and rev it as hard as you can."

A Wonderful Life

Peter never imagined that smashing his thumb in a car door would be the best thing to ever happened to him. But suddenly his plans to move in to the dorm were changed, and he waited a long time at the hospital before finally returning to the dorm and moving in.

Peter arrived for the second time well after check-in time, praying to be able to get in. After a few phone calls, a security officer came in, expressed sympathy about his bandaged thumb, and let him up to his room. The family moved his possessions from the car to his room and made his bed in a few minutes, and by the time it was down, the security guard had called the RA, who brought Peter his keys.

It was the wee hours of the morning when Peter looked at his new home for the second time, and tough as Peter was, the pain in his thumb kept him from falling asleep. He was in as much pain as he'd been in for a while.

He awoke when the light was ebbing, and after some preparations set out, wandering until he found the cafeteria. The pain seemed much when he sat down at a table. (It took him a while to find a seat because the cafeteria was crowded.)

A young man said, "Hi, I'm John." Peter began to extend his hand, then looked at his white bandaged thumb and said, "Excuse me for not shaking your hand. I am Peter."

A young woman said, "I'm Mary. I saw you earlier and was hoping to see you more."

Peter wondered about something, then said, "I'll drink for that," reached with his right hand, grabbed a glass of soda, and then winced in pain, spilling his drink on the table.

Everybody at the table moved. A couple of people dodged the flow of liquid; others stopped what they were doing, rushing to mop up the spill with napkins. Peter said, "I keep forgetting I need to be careful about my thumb," smiled, grabbed his glass of milk, and slipped again, spilling milk all over his food.

Peter stopped, sat back, and then laughed for a while. "This is an interesting beginning to my college education."

Mary said, "I noticed you managed to smash your thumb in a car door without saying any words you regret. What else has happened?"

Peter said, "Nothing great; I had to go to the ER, where I had to wait, before they could do something about my throbbing thumb. I got back at 4:00 AM and couldn't get to sleep for a long time because I was in so much pain. Then I overslept my alarm and woke up naturally in time for dinner. How about you?"

Mary thought for a second about the people she met. Peter could see the sympathy on her face.

John said, "Wow. That's nasty."

Peter said, "I wish we couldn't feel pain. Have you thought about how nice it would be to live without pain?"

Mary said, "I'd like that."

John said, "Um..."

Mary said, "What?"

John said, "Actually, there are people who don't feel pain, and there's a name for the condition. You've heard of it."

Peter said, "I haven't heard of that before."

John said, "Yes you have. It's called leprosy."

Peter said, "What do you mean by 'leprosy'? I thought leprosy was a disease that ravaged the body."

John said, "It is. But that is only because it destroys the ability to feel pain. The way it works is very simple. We all get little nicks and scratches, and because they hurt, we show extra sensitivity. Our feet start to hurt after a long walk, so without even thinking about it we... shift things a little, and keep anything really bad from happening. That pain you are feeling is your body's way of asking room to heal so that the smashed thumbnail (or whatever it is) that hurts so terribly now won't leave you permanently maimed. Back to feet, a leprosy patient will walk exactly the same way and get wounds we'd never even think of for taking a long walk. All the terrible injuries that make leprosy a feared disease happen *only* because leprosy keeps people from feeling pain."

Peter looked at his thumb, and his stomach growled.

John said, "I'm full. Let me get a drink for you, and then I'll help you drink it."

Mary said, "And I'll get you some dry food. We've already eaten; it must—"

Peter said, "Please, I've survived much worse. It's just a bit of pain."

John picked up a clump of wet napkins and threatened to throw it at Peter before standing up and walking to get something to drink. Mary followed him.

Peter sat back and just laughed.

John said, "We have some time free after dinner; let's just wander around campus."

They left the glass roofed building and began walking around, enjoying the grass and the scenery.

After some wandering, Peter and those he had just met looked at the castle-like Blanchard Hall, each one transported in his imagination to be in a more ancient era, and walked around the campus, looked at a fountain, listened to some music, and looked at a display of a giant mastodon which had died before the end of the last ice age, and whose bones had been unearthed in a nearby excavation. They got lost, but this was not a terrible concern; they were taking in the campus.

Their slow walk was interrupted when John looked at his watch and realized it was time for the "floor fellowship." and orientation games.

Between orientation games, Peter heard bits of conversation: "This has been a bummer; I've gotten two papercuts this week." "—and then I—" "What instruments do you—" "I'm from France too! *Tu viens de Paris?*" "Really? You—" Everybody seemed to be chattering, and Peter wished he could be in one of—actually, several of those conversations at once.

Paul's voice cut in and said, "For this next activity we are going to form a human circle. With your team, stand in a circle, and everybody reach in and grab another hand with each hand. Then hold on tight; when I say, "Go," you want to untangle yourselves, without letting go. The first team to untangle themselves wins!"

Peter reached in, and found each of his hands clasped in a solid, masculine grip. Then the race began, and people jostled and tried to untangle themselves. This was a laborious process and, one by one, every other group freed itself, while Peter's group seemed stuck on—someone called and said, "I think we're knotted!" As people began to thin out, Paul looked with astonishment and saw that they were indeed knotted. "A special prize to them, too, for managing the best tangle!"

"And now, we'll have a three-legged race! Gather into pairs, and each two of you take a burlap sack. Then—" Paul continued, and with every game, the talk seemed to flow more. When the finale finished, Peter found himself again with John and Mary and heard the conversations flowing around him: "Really? You too?" "But you don't understand. Hicks have a slower pace of life; we enjoy things without all the things you city dwellers need for entertainment. And we learn resourceful ways to—" "—and only at Wheaton would the administration *forbid* dancing while *requiring* the games we just played and—" Then Peter lost himself in a conversation that continued long into the night. He expected to be up at night thinking about all the beloved people he left at home, but Peter was too busy thinking about John's and Mary's stories.

The next day Peter woke up his to the hideous sound of his alarm clock, and groggily trudged to the dining hall for coffee, and searched for his advisor.

Peter found the appropriate hallway, wandered around nervously until he found a door with a yellowed plaque that said "Julian Johnson," knocked once, and pushed the door open. A white-haired man said, "Peter Jones? How are you? Do come in... What can I do for you?"

Peter pulled out a sheet of paper, looked down at it for a moment and said, "I'm sorry I'm late. I need you to write what courses I should take and sign here. Then I can be out of your way."

The old man sat back, drew a deep breath, and relaxed into a fatherly smile. Peter began to wonder if his advisor was going to say anything at all. Then Prof. Johnson motioned towards an armchair, as rich and luxurious as his own, and then looked as if he remembered something and offered a bowl full of candy. "Sit down, sit down, and make yourself comfortable. May I interest you in candy?" He picked up an engraved metal bowl and held it out while Peter grabbed a few Lifesavers.

Prof. Johnson sat back, silent for a moment, and said, "I'm sorry I'm out of butterscotch; that always seems to disappear. Please sit down, and tell me about yourself. We can get to that form in a minute. One of the priveleges of this job is that I get to meet interesting people. Now, where are you from?"

Peter said, "I'm afraid there's not much that's interesting about me. I'm from a small town downstate that doesn't have anything to distinguish itself. My amusements have been reading, watching the cycle of the year, oh, and running. Not much interesting in that. Now which classes should I take?"

Prof. Johnson sat back and smiled, and Peter became a little less tense. "You run?"

Peter said, "Yes; I was hoping to run on the track this afternoon, after the lecture. I've always wanted to run on a real track."

The old man said, "You know, I used to run myself, before I became an official Old Geezer and my orthopaedist told me my knees couldn't take it. So I have to content myself with swimming now, which I've grown to love. Do you know about the Prairie Path?"

Peter said, "No, what's that?"

Prof. Johnson said, "Years ago, when I ran, I ran through the areas surrounding the College—there are a lot of beautiful houses. And, just south of the train tracks with the train you can hear now, there's a path before you even hit the street. You can run, or bike, or walk, on a path covered with fine white gravel, with trees and prairie plants on either side. It's a lovely view." He paused, and said, "Any ideas what you want to do after Wheaton?"

Peter said, "No. I don't even know what I want to major in."

Prof. Johnson said, "A lot of students don't know what they want to do. Are you familiar with Career Services? They can help you get an idea of what kinds of things you like to do."

Peter looked at his watch and said, "It's chapel time."

Prof. Johnson said, "Relax. I can write you a note." Peter began to relax again, and Prof. Johnson continued, "Now you like to read. What do you like to read?"

Peter said, "Newspapers and magazines, and I read this really cool book called *Zen and the Art of Motorcycle Maintenance*. Oh, and I like the Bible."

Prof. Johnson said, "I do too. What do you like about it most?"

"I like the stories in the Old Testament."

"One general tip: here at Wheaton, we have different kinds of professors—"

Peter said, "Which ones are best?"

Prof. Johnson said, "Different professors are best for different students. Throughout your tenure at Wheaton, ask your friends and learn which professors have teaching styles that you learn well with and mesh well with. Consider taking other courses from a professor you like. Now we have a lot of courses which we think expose you to new things and stretch you—people come back and see that these courses are best. Do you like science?"

"I like it; I especially liked a physics lab."

Prof. Johnson began to flip through the course catalogue. "Have you had calculus?" Prof. Johnson's mind wandered over the differences between from the grand, Utopian vision for "calculus" as it was first imagined and how different a conception it had from anything that would be considered "mathematics" today. Or should he go into that? He wavered, and then realized Peter had answered his question. "Ok," Prof. Johnson said, "the lab physics class unfortunately requires that you've had calculus. Would you like to take calculus now? Have you had geometry, algebra, and trigonometry?"

Peter said, "Yes, I did, but I'd like a little break from that now. Maybe I could take calculus next semester."

"Fair enough. You said you liked to read."

"Magazines and newspapers."

"Those things deal with the unfolding human story. I wonder if you'd like to take world civilization now, or a political science course."

"History, but why study world history? Why can't I just study U.S. history?"

Prof. Johnson said, "The story of our country is intertwined with that of our world. I think you might find that some of the things in world history are a lot closer to home than you think—and we have some real storytellers in our history department."

"That sounds interesting. What else?"

"The Theology of Culture class is one many students find enjoyable, and it helps build a foundation for Old and New Testament courses. Would you be interested in taking it for A quad or B quad, the first or second half of the semester?"

"Could I do both?"

"I wish I could say yes, but this course only lasts half the semester. The other half you could take Foundations of Wellness—you could do running as homework!"

"I think I'll do that first, and then Theology of Culture. That should be new," Peter said, oblivious to how tightly connected he was to theology and culture. "What else?"

Prof. Johnson said, "We have classes where people read things that a lot of people have found really interesting. Well, that could describe several classes, but I was thinking about Classics of Western Literature or Literature of the Modern World."

Peter said, "Um... Does Classics of Western Literature cover ancient and medieval literature, and Literature of the Modern World cover literature that isn't Western? Because if they do, I'm not sure I could connect with it."

Prof. Johnson relaxed into his seat. "You know, a lot of people think that. But you know what?"

Peter said, "What?"

"There is something human that crosses cultures. That is why the stories have been selected. Stories written long ago, and stories written far away, can have a lot to connect with."

"Ok. How many more courses should I take?"

"You're at 11 credits now; you probably want 15. Now you said that you like *Zen and the Art of Motorcycle Maintenance*. I'm wondering if you would also like a philosophy course."

Peter said, "*Zen and the Art of Motorcycle Maintenance* is... I don't suppose there are any classes that use that. Or are there? I've heard Pirsig isn't given his fair due by philosophers."

Prof. Johnson said, "If you approach one of our philosophy courses the way you approach *Zen and the Art of Motorcycle Maintenance*, I think you'll profit from the encounter. I wonder if our Issues and Worldviews in Philosophy might interest you. I'm a big fan of thinking worldviewishly, and our philosophers have some pretty interesting things to say."

Peter asked, "What does 'worldviewishly' mean?"

Prof. Johnson searched for an appropriate simplification. "It means thinking in terms of worldviews. A worldview is the basic philosophical framework that gives shape to how we view the world. Our philosophers will be able to help you understand the basic issues surrounding worldviews and craft your own Christian worldview. You may find this frees you from the Enlightenment's secularizing influence—and if you don't know what the Enlightenment is now, you will learn to understand it, and its problems, and how you can be somewhat freer of its chain."

Peter said, "Ok. Well, I'll take those classes. It was good to meet you."

Prof. Johnson looked at the class schedule and helped Peter choose class sections, then said, "I enjoyed talking with you. Please do take some more candy—put a handful in your pocket or something. I just want to make one more closing comment. I want to see you succeed. Wheaton wants to see you succeed. There are some rough points and problems along the way, and if you bring them to me I can work with them and try to help you. If you want to talk with your RA or our chaplain or someone else, that's fine, but please... my door is *always* open. And it was good to meet you too! Goodbye!"

Peter walked out, completely relaxed, and was soon to be energized in a scavenger hunt searching for things from a dog biscuit to a car bumper to a burning sheet of paper not lit by someone in his group, before again relaxing into the "brother-sister floor fellowship" which combined mediocre "7-11 praise songs" (so called because they have "7 words, repeated 11 times") with the light of another world shining through.

It was not long before the opening activities wound down and Peter began to settle into a regular routine.

Peter and Mary both loved to run, but for different reasons. Peter was training himself for various races; he had not joined track, as he did in high school, but there were other races. Mary ran to feel the sun and wind and rain. And, without any conscious effort, they found themselves running together down the prairie path together, and Peter clumsily learning to match his speed to hers. And, as time passed, they talked, and talked, and talked, and talked, and their runs grew longer.

When the fall break came, they both joined a group going to the northwoods of Wisconsin for a program that was half-work and half-play. And each one wrote a letter home about the other. Then Peter began his theology of culture class, and said, "This is what I want to study." Mary did not have a favorite class, at least not that she realized, until Peter asked her what her favorite class was and she said, "Literature."

When Christmas came, they went to their respective homes and spent the break thinking about each other, and they talked about this when they returned. They ended the conversation, or at least they thought they did, and then each hurried back to catch the other and say one more thing, and then the conversation turned out to last much longer, and ended with a kiss.

Valentine's Day was syrupy. It was trite enough that their more romantically inclined friends groaned, but it did not seem at all trite or syrupy to them. As Peter's last name was Patrick, he called Mary's father and prayed that St. Patrick's Day would be a momentous day for both of them.

Peter and Mary took a slow run to a nearby village, and

had dinner at an Irish pub. Amidst the din, they had some hearty laughs. The waitress asked Mary, "Is there anything else that would make this night memorable?" Then Mary saw Peter on his knee, opening a jewelry box with a ring: "I love you, Mary. Will you marry me?"

Mary cried for a good five minutes before she could answer. And when she had answered, they sat in silence, a silence that overpowered the din. Then Mary wiped her eyes and they went outside.

It was cool outside, and the moon was shining brightly. Peter pulled a camera from his pocket, and said, "Stay where you are. Let me back up a bit. And hold your hand up. You look even more beautiful with that ring on your finger."

Peter's camera flashed as he took a picture, just as a drunk driver slammed into Mary. The sedan spun into a storefront, and Mary flew up into the air, landed, and broke a beer bottle with her face.

People began to come out, and in a few minutes the police and paramedics arrived. Peter somehow managed to answer the police officers' questions and to begin kicking himself for being too stunned to act.

When Peter left his room the next day, he looked for Prof. Johnson. Prof. Johnson asked, "May I give you a hug?" and then sat there, simply being with Peter in his pain. When Peter left, Prof. Johnson said, "I'm not just here for academics. I'm here for you." Peter went to chapel and his classes, feeling a burning rage that almost nothing could pierce. He kept going to the hospital, and watching Mary with casts on both legs and one arm, and many tiny stitches on her face, fluttering on the borders of consciousness. One time Prof. Johnson came to visit, and he said, "I can't finish my classes." Prof. Johnson looked at him and said, "The college will give you a full refund." Peter said, "Do you know of any way I can stay here to be with Mary?" Prof. Johnson said, "You can stay with me. And I believe a position with UPS would let you get some income, doing something physical. The position is open for you." Prof. Johnson didn't mention the calls he'd made, and Peter didn't think about them. He simply said, "Thank you."

A few days later, Mary began to be weakly conscious. Peter finally asked a nurse, "Why are there so many stitches on her face? Was she cut even more badly than—"

The nurse said, "There are a lot of stitches very close together because the emergency room had a cosmetic surgeon on duty. There will still be a permanent mark on her face, but some of the wound will heal without a scar."

Mary moved the left half of her mouth in half a smile. Peter said, "That was a kind of cute smile. How come she can smile like that?"

The nurse said, "One of the pieces of broken glass cut a nerve. It is unlikely she'll ever be able to move part of her face again."

Peter looked and touched Mary's hand. "I still think it's really quite cute."

Mary looked at him, and then passed out.

Peter spent a long couple of days training and attending to practical details. Then he came back to Mary.

Mary looked at Peter, and said, "It's a Monday. Don't you have classes now?"

Peter said, "No."

Mary said, "Why not?"

Peter said, "I want to be here with you."

Mary said, "I talked with one of the nurses, and she said that you dropped out of school so you could be with me.

"Is that true?" she said.

Peter said, "I hadn't really thought about it that way."

Mary closed her eyes, and when Peter started to leave because he decided she wanted to be left alone, she said, "Stop. Come here."

Peter came to her bedside and knelt.

Mary said, "Take this ring off my finger."

Peter said, "Is it hurting you?"

Mary said, "No, and it is the greatest treasure I own.

Take it off and take it back."

Peter looked at her, bewildered. "Do you not want to marry me?"

Mary said, "This may sting me less because I don't remember our engagement. I don't remember anything that happened near that time; I have only the stories others, even the nurses, tell me about a man who loves me very much."

Peter said, "But don't you love me?"

Mary forced back tears. "Yes, I love you, yes, I love you. And I know that you love me. You are young and strong, and have the love to make a happy marriage. You'll make some woman a very good husband. I thought that woman would be me.

"But I can see what you will not. You said I was beautiful, and I was. Do you know what my prognosis is? I will probably be able to stand. At least for short periods of time. If I'm fortunate, I may walk. With a walker. I will never be able to run again—Peter, I am nobody, and I have no future. Absolutely nobody. You are young and strong. Go and find a woman who is worth your love."

Mary and Peter both cried for a long time. Then Peter walked out, and paused in the doorway, crying. He felt torn inside, and then went in to say a couple of things to Mary. He said, "I believe in miracles."

Then Mary cried, and Peter said something else I'm not going to repeat. Mary said something. Then another conversation began.

The conversation ended with Mary saying, "You're stupid, Peter. You're really, really stupid. I love you. I don't deserve such love. You're making a mistake. I love you." Then Peter went to kiss Mary, and as he bent down, he bent his mouth to meet the lips that he still saw as "really quite cute."

The stress did not stop. The physical therapists, after time, wondered that Mary had so much fight in her. But it stressed her, and Peter did his job without liking it. Mary and Peter quarreled and made up and quarreled and made up. Peter prayed for a miracle when they made up and sometimes when they quarreled. Were this not enough stress, there was an agonizingly long trial—and knowing that the drunk driver was behind bars didn't make things better. But Mary very slowly learned to walk again. After six months, if Peter helped her, she could walk 100 yards before the pain became too great to continue.

Peter hadn't been noticing that the stress diminished, but he did become aware of something he couldn't put his finger on. After a night of struggling, he got up, went to church, and was floored by the Bible reading of, "You have heard that it was said, 'Love your neighbor and hate your enemy.' But I tell you, love your enemies and pray for those who persecute you." and the idea that when you do or do not visit someone in prison, you are visiting or refusing to visit Christ. Peter absently went home, tried to think about other things, made several phone calls, and then forced himself to drive to one and only one prison.

He stopped in the parking lot, almost threw up, and then steeled himself to go inside. He found a man, Jacob, and... Jacob didn't know who Peter was, but he recognized him as looking familiar. It was an awkward meeting. Then he recognized him as the man whose now wife he had crippled. When Peter left, he vomited and felt like a failure. He talked about it with Mary...

That was the beginning of a friendship. Peter chose to love the man in prison, even if there was no pleasure in it. And that created something deeper than pleasure, something Peter couldn't explain.

As Peter and Mary were planning the wedding, Mary said, "I want to enter with Peter next to me, no matter what the tradition says. It will be a miracle if I have the strength to stand for the whole wedding, and if I have to lean on someone I want it to be Peter. And I don't want to sit on a chair; I would rather spend my wedding night wracked by pain than go through my wedding supported by something lifeless!"

When the rehearsal came, Mary stood, and the others winced at the pain in her face. And she stood, and walked, for the entire rehearsal without touching Peter once. Then she said, "I can do it. I can go through the wedding on my own strength," and collapsed in pain.

At the wedding, she stood next to Peter, walking, her face so radiant with joy that some of the guests did not guess she was in exquisite pain. They walked next to each other, not touching, and Mary slowed down and stopped in the center of the church. Peter looked at her, wondering what Mary was doing.

Then Mary's arm shot around Peter's neck, and Peter stood startled for a moment before he placed his arm around her, squeezed her tightly, and they walked together to the altar.

On the honeymoon, Mary told Peter, "You are the only person I need." This was the greatest bliss either of them had known, and the honeymoon's glow shined and shined.

Peter and Mary agreed to move somewhere less expensive to settle down, and were too absorbed in their wedded bliss and each other to remember promises they had made earlier, promises to seek a church community for support and friends. And Peter continued working at an unglamorous job, and Mary continued fighting to walk and considered the housework she was capable of doing a badge of honor, and neither of them noticed that the words, "I love you" were spoken ever so slightly less frequently, nor did they the venom and ice creeping into their words.

One night they exploded. What they fought about was not important. What was important was that Peter left, burning with rage. He drove, and drove, until he reached Wheaton, and at daybreak knocked on Prof. Johnson's door. There was anger in his voice when he asked, "Are you still my friend?"

Prof. Johnson got him something to eat and stayed with him when he fumed with rage, and said, "I don't care if I'm supposed to be with her, I can't go back!" Then Prof. Johnson said, "Will you make an agreement with me? I promise you I won't ever tell you to go back to her, or accept her, or accept what she does, or apologize to her, or forgive her, or in any way be reconciled. But I need you to trust me that I love you and will help you decide what is best to do."

Peter said, "Yes."

Prof. Johnson said, "Then stay with me. You need some rest. Take the day to rest. There's food in the fridge, and I have books and a nice back yard. There's iced tea in the— excuse me, there's Coke and 7 Up in the boxes next to the fridge. When I can come back, we can talk."

Peter relaxed, and he felt better. He told Prof. Johnson. Prof. Johnson said, "That's excellent. What I'd like you to do next is go in to work, with a lawyer I know. You can tell him what's going on, and he'll lead you to a courtroom to observe."

Peter went away to court the next day, and when he came back he was ashen. He said nothing to Prof. Johnson.

Then, after the next day, he came back looking even more disturbed. "The first day, the lawyer, George, took me into divorce court. I thought I saw the worst that divorce court could get. Until I came back today. It was the same— this sickening scene where two people had become the most bitter enemies. I hope it doesn't come to this. This was atrocious. It was vile. It was more than vile. It was—"

Prof. Johnson sent him back for a third day. This time Peter said nothing besides, "I think I've been making a mistake."

After the fourth day, Peter said, "Help me! I've been making the biggest mistake of my *life*!"

After a full week had passed, Peter said, "*Please*, I *beg* you, don't send me back there."

Prof. Johnson sent Peter back to watch a divorce court for one more miserable, excruciating day. Then he said, "Now you can do whatever you want. What do you want to do?"

The conflict between Peter and Mary ended the next day.

Peter went home, begging Mary for forgiveness, and no sooner than he had begun his apology, a thousand things were reflected in Mary's face and she begged his forgiveness. Then they talked, and debated whether to go back to Wheaton, or stay where they were. Finally Mary said, "I really want to go back to Wheaton."

Peter began to shyly approach old friends. He later misquoted: "I came crawling with a thimble in the desparate hope that they'd give a few tiny drops of friendship and love. Had I known how they would respond, I would have come running with a bucket!"

Peter and Mary lived together for many years; they had many children and were supported by many friends.

The years passed and Peter and Mary grew into a blissfully happy marriage. Mary came to have increasing health problems as a result of the accident, and those around them were amazed at how their love had transformed the suffering the accident created in both of their lives. At least those who knew them best saw the transformation. There were many others who could only see their happiness as a mirage.

As the years passed, Jacob grew to be a good friend. And when Peter began to be concerned that his wife might be... Jacob had also grown wealthy, very wealthy, and assembled a top-flight legal team (without taking a dime of Peter's money—over Peter's protests, of course), to prevent what the doctors would normally do in such a case, given recent shifts in the medical system.

And then Mary's health grew worse, much worse, and her suffering grew worse with it, and pain medications seemed to be having less and less effect. Those who didn't know Mary were astonished that someone in so much pain could enjoy life so much, nor the hours they spent gazing into each other's eyes, holding hands, when Mary's pain seemed to vanish. A second medical opinion, and a third, and a fourth, confirmed that Mary had little chance of recovery even to her more recent state. And whatever measures been taken, whatever testimony Peter and Mary could give about the joy of their lives, the court's decision still came:

> The court wishes to briefly review the facts of the case. Subject is suffering increasingly severe effects from an injury that curtailed her life greatly as a young person. from which she has never recovered, and is causing increasingly complications now that she will never again have youth's ability to heal. No fewer than four medical opinions admitted as expert testimony substantially agree that subject is in extraordinary and excruciating pain; that said excruciating pain is increasing; that said excruciating pain is increasingly unresponsive to medication; that subject has fully lost autonomy and is dependent on her husband; that this dependence is profound, without choice, and causes her husband to be dependent without choice on others and exercise little autonomy; and the prognosis is only of progressively worse deterioration and increase in pain, with no question of recovery.
>
> The court finds it entirely understandable that the subject, who has gone through such trauma, and is suffering increasingly severe complications, would be in a state of some denial. Although a number of positions could be taken, the court also finds it understandable that a husband would try to maintain a hold on what cannot exist, and needlessly prolong his wife's suffering. It is not, however, the court's position to judge whether this is selfish...
>
> For all the impressive-sounding arguments that have been mounted, the court cannot accord a traumatized patient or her ostensibly well-meaning husband a privelege that the court itself does not claim. The court does not find that it has an interest in

allowing this woman to continue in her severe and worsening state of suffering.

Peter was at her side, holding her hand and looking into his wife's eyes, The hospital doctor had come. Then Peter said, "I love you," and Mary said, "I love you," and they kissed.

Mary's kiss was still burning on Peter's lips when two nurses hooked Mary up to an IV and injected her with 5000 milligrams of sodium thiopental, then a saline flush followed by 100 milligrams of pancurium bromide, then a saline flush and 20 milligrams of potassium chloride.

A year later to the day, Peter died of a broken heart.

Within the Steel Orb

The car pulled up on the dark cobblestones and stopped by the darker castle. The vehicle was silver-grey, low to the ground, and sleek. A—let us call him a man—opened the driver's door on the right, and stood up, tall, dark, clad in a robe the color of the sky at midnight. Around the car he went, opened the door for his passenger, and once the passenger stepped out, made one swift motion and had two bags on his shoulder. The bags were large, but he moved as if he were accustomed to carrying far heavier fare. It was starlight out, and the moon was visible as moonlight rippled across a pool.

The guest reached for the bags. "Those are heavy. Let me—"

The host smiled darkly. "Do not worry about the weight of your bags."

The host opened a solid greyblack door, of unearthly smoothness, and walked swiftly down a granite hallway, allowing his guest to follow. "You've had a long day. Let me get you something to drink." He turned a door, poured something into two iridescent titanium mugs, and turned through another corridor and opened a door on its side. Inside the room were two deep armchairs and a low table.

"This is my first time traveling between worlds—how am I to address you?"

The host smiled. "Why do you wish to know more of my name? It is enough for you to call me Oinos. Please enjoy our welcome."

The guest sipped his drink. "Cider?"

The host said, "You may call it that; it is a juice, which has not had artificial things done to make it taste like it just came out of its fruit regardless of how much it should have aged by the time you taste it. It is juice where time has been allowed to do its work." He was holding a steel orb. "You are welcome here, Art." Then—he barely seemed to move— there was a spark, and Oinos pulled a candle from the wall and set it on the table.

Art said, "Why not a fluorescent light to really light the room up?"

The host said, "For the same reason that you either do not offer your guests mocha at all, or else give them real mocha and not a mix of hot water, instant coffee, and hot cocoa powder. In our world, we can turn the room bright as day any time, but we do not often do so."

"Aah. We have a lot to learn from you about getting back to nature."

"Really? What do you mean by 'getting back to nature'? What do you do to try to 'get back to nature'?"

"Um, I don't know what to really do. Maybe try to be in touch with the trees, not being cooped up inside all the time, if I were doing a better job of it..."

"If that is getting back in touch with nature, then we pay little attention to getting in touch with nature. And nature, as we understand it, is about something fundamentally beyond dancing on hills or sitting and watching waves. I don't criticize you if you do them, but there is really something more. And I can talk with you about drinking juice without touching the natural processes that make cider or what have you, and I can talk with you about natural cycles and why we don't have imitation daylight any time it would seem convenient. But I would like you to walk away with something more, and more interesting, than how we keep technology from being too disruptive to natural processes. That isn't really the point. It's almost what you might call a side effect."

"But you do an awfully impressive job of putting technology in its place and not getting too involved with it."

Oinos said, "Have you had enough chance to stretch out and rest and quench your thirst? Would you like to see something?"

"Yes."

Oinos stood, and led the way down some stairs to a room that seemed to be filled with odd devices. He pushed some things aside, then walked up to a device with a square in the center, and pushed one side. Chains and gears moved, and another square replaced it.

"This is my workshop, with various items that I have worked on. You can come over here and play with this little labyrinth; it's not completely working, but you can explore it if you take the time to figure it out. Come on over. It's what I've been working on most recently."

Art looked around, somewhat amazed, and walked over to the 'labyrinth.'

Oinos said, "In your world, in classical Greek, the same word, 'techne,' means both 'art' and 'technology.' You misunderstand my kindred if you think we aren't especially interested in technology; we have a great interest in technology, as with other kinds of art. But just as you can travel a long distance to see the Mona Lisa without needing a mass-produced Mona Lisa to hang in your bathroom, we enjoy and appreciate technologies without making them conveniences we need to have available every single day."

Art pressed a square and the labyrinth shifted. "Have I come here to see technologies?"

Oinos paused. "I would not advise it. You see our technologies, or how we use them, because that is what you are most ready to see. Visitors from some other worlds hardly notice them, even if they are astonished when they are pointed out."

Art said, "Then why don't we go back to the other room?"

Oinos turned. "Excellent." They went back, and Art sat down in his chair.

Art, after a long pause, said, "I still find it puzzling why, if you appreciate technology, you don't want to have more of it."

Oinos said, "Why do you find it so puzzling?"

"Technology *does* seem to add a lot to the body."

"That is a very misleading way to put it. The effect of most technologies that you think of as adding to the body is in fact to undercut the body. The technologies that you call 'space-conquering' might be appropriately called 'body-conquering.'"

"So the telephone is a body-conquering device? Does it make my body less real?"

"Once upon a time, long ago from your perspective, news and information could not really travel faster than a person could travel. If you were talking with a person, that person had to be pretty close, and it was awkward and inconvenient to communicate with those who were far away. That meant that the people you talked with were probably people from your local community."

"So you were deprived of easy access to people far away?"

"Let me put it this way. It mattered where you were, meaning where your body was. Now, on the telephone, or instant messages, or the web, nothing and no one is really anywhere, and that means profound things for what communities are. And are not. You may have read about 'close-knit rural communities' which have become something exotic and esoteric to most of your world's city dwellers... but when space conquering technologies had not come in, and another space-conquering technology, modern roads allowing easy moving so that people would have to say goodbye to face-to-face friendships every few years... It's a very different way of relating. A close-knit rural community is exotic to you because it is a body-based community in ways that tend not to happen when people make heavy use of body-conquering, or space-conquering, or whatever you want to call them, technologies."

"But isn't there more than a lack of technologies to close-knit communities?"

"Yes, indeed... but... spiritual discipline is about much more than the body, but a lot of spiritual discipline can only shape people when people are running into the body's limitations. The disciplines—worship, prayer, fasting, silence, almsgiving, and so on—only mean something if there are bodily limits you are bumping into. If you can take a pill that takes away your body's discomfort in fasting, or standing through worship, then the body-conquering technology of that pill has cut you off from the spiritual benefit of that practice."

"Aren't spiritual practices about more than the body?"

"Yes indeed, but you won't get there if you have something less than the body."

Art sat back. "I'd be surprised if you're not a real scientist. I imagine that in your world you know things that our scientists will not know for centuries."

Oinos sat back and sat still for a time, closing his eyes. Then he opened his eyes and said, "What have you learned from science?"

"I've spent a lot of time lately, wondering what Einstein's theory of relativity means for us today: even the 'hard' sciences are relative, and what 'reality' is, depends greatly on your own perspective. Even in the hardest sciences, it is fundamentally mistaken to be looking for absolute truth."

Oinos leaned forward, paused, and then tapped the table four different places. In front of Art appeared a gridlike object which Art recognized with a start as a scientific calculator like his son's. "Very well. Let me ask you a question. Relative to your frame of reference, an object of one kilogram rest mass is moving away from you at a speed of one tenth the speed of light. What, from your present frame of reference, is its effective mass?"

Art hesitated, and began to sit up.

Oinos said, "If you'd prefer, the table can be set to function as any major brand of calculator you're familiar with. Or would you prefer a computer with Matlab or Mathematica? The remainder of the table's surface can be used to browse the appropriate manuals."

Art shrunk slightly towards his chair.

Oinos said, "I'll give you hints. In the theory of relativity, objects can have an effective mass of above their rest mass, but never below it. Furthermore, most calculations of this type tend to have anything that changes, change by a factor of the inverse of the square root of the quantity: one minus the square of the object's speed divided by the square of the speed of light. Do you need me to explain the buttons on the calculator?"

Art shrunk into his chair. "I don't know all of those technical details, but I have spent a lot of time thinking about relativity."

Oinos said, "If you are unable to answer that question before I started dropping hints, let alone after I gave hints, you should not pose as having contemplated what relativity means for us today. I'm not trying to humiliate you. But the first question I asked is the kind of question a teacher would put on a quiz to see if students were awake and not playing video games for most of the first lecture. I know it's fashionable in your world to drop Einstein's name as someone you have deeply pondered. It is also extraordinarily silly. I have noticed that scientists who have a good understanding of relativity often work without presenting themselves as having these deep ponderings about what Einstein means for them today. Trying to deeply ponder Einstein without learning even the basics of relativistic physics is like trying to write the next Nobel prize-winning German novel without being bothered to learn even them most rudimentary German vocabulary and grammar."

"But don't you think that relativity makes a big difference?"

"On a poetic level, I think it is an interesting development in your world's history for a breakthrough in science, Einstein's theory of relativity, to say that what is absolute is not time, but light. Space and time bend before light. There is a poetic beauty to Einstein making an unprecedented absolute out of light. But let us leave poetic appreciation of Einstein's theory aside.

"You might be interested to know that the differences predicted by Einstein's theory of relativity are so minute that decades passed between Einstein making the theory of relativity and people being able to use a sensitive enough clock to measure the minute difference of the so-called 'twins paradox' by bringing an atomic clock on an airplane. The answer to the problem I gave you is that for a tenth the speed of light—which is faster than you can imagine, and well over a thousand times the top speed of the fastest supersonic vehicle your world will ever make—is one half of one percent. It's a disappointingly small increase for a rather astounding speed. If the supersonic Skylon is ever built, would you care to guess the increase in effective mass as it travels at an astounding Mach 5.5?"

"Um, I don't know..."

"Can you guess? Half its mass? The mass of a car? Or just the mass of a normal-sized adult?"

"Is this a trick question? Fifty pounds?"

"The effective mass increases above the rest mass, for that massive vehicle running at about five times the speed of sound and almost twice the top speed of the SR-71 Blackbird, is something like the mass of a mosquito."

"A *mosquito*? You're joking, right?"

"No. It's an underwhelming, *microscopic* difference for what relativity says when the rumor mill has it that Einstein taught us that hard sciences are as fuzzy as anything else... or that perhaps, in Star Wars terms, 'Luke, you're going to find that many of the truths we cling to depend greatly on your own point of view.' Under Einstein, you will in fact **not** find that many of the observations that we cling to, depend greatly on your own frame of reference. You have to be doing something pretty exotic to have relativity make any measurable difference from the older physics at all."

"Would you explain relativity to me so that I can discuss its implications?"

"I really think there might be more productive ways to use your visit."

"But you have a scientist's understanding of relativity."

"I am not sure I'd say that."

"Why? You seem to understand relativity a lot more like a scientist than I do."

"Let's talk about biology for a moment. Do you remember the theory of spontaneous generation? You know, the theory that life just emerges from appropriate material?"

"I think so."

"But your world's scientists haven't believed in spontaneous generation since over a century before you were born. Why would you be taught that theory—I'm assuming you learned this in a science class and not digging into history?"

"My science course explained the theory in covering historical background, even though scientists no longer believe that bread spontaneously generates mold."

"Let me ask what may seem like a non-sequitur. I assume you're familiar with people who are working to get even more of religion taken out of public schools?"

"Yes."

"They are very concerned about official prayers at school events, right? About having schools endorse even the occasional religious practice?"

"Yes."

"Ok. Let me ask what may seem like a strange question. Have these 'separation of Church and state' advocates also advocated that geometry be taken out of the classroom?"

Art closed his eyes, and then looked at Oinos as if he had two heads. "It seems you don't know everything about my world."

"I don't. But please understand that geometry did not originate as a secular technical practice. You migth have heard this mentioned. Geometry began its life as a 'sacred science,' or a religious practice, and to its founders the idea that geometry does not have religious content would have struck them as worse than saying that prayer does not have religious content."

"Ok, I think I remember that being mentioned. So to speak, my math teacher taught about geometry the 'sacred science' the way that my biology teacher taught about the past theory of spontaneous generation."

Oinos focused his eyes on Art. "In our schools, and in our training, physics, biology, and chemistry are 'taught' as 'secular sciences' the same way, in your school, spontaneous generation is taught as 'past science', or even better, the 'sacred science' of geometry is 'taught' in the course of getting on to a modern understanding of geometry."

Art said, "So the idea that the terrain we call 'biology' is to you—"

Oinos continued: "As much something peered at through a glass bell as the idea that the terrain of regular polygons belongs to a secularized mathematics."

"What is a sacred science?"

Oinos sat back. "If a science is about understanding something as self-contained whose explanations do not involve God, and it is an attempt to understand as physics understand, and the scientist understands as a detached observer, looking in through a window, then you have a secular science—the kind that reeks of the occult to us. Or that may sound strange, because in your world people proclaiming sacred sciences are proclaiming the occult. But let me deal with that later. A sacred science does not try to understand objects as something that can be explained without reference to God. A sacred science is first and foremost about God, not about objects. When it understands objects, it understands them out of God, and tries to see God shining through them. A sacred science has its home base in the understanding of God, not of inanimate matter, and its understanding of things bears the imprint of God. If you want the nature of its knowing in an image, do not think of someone looking in and observing, detached, through a window, but someone drinking something in."

"Is everything a sacred science to you? And what is a sacred science? Astrology?"

"Something like that, except that I use the term 'sacred science' by way of accommodation. Our own term is one that has no good translation in your language. But let us turn to the stars."

"Astrology is right in this: a star is more than a ball of plasma. Even in the Bible there is not always such a distinction between the ranks of angels and the stars as someone raised on materialist science might think." He rose, and began to walk, gesturing for Art to follow him. In the passage, they turned and entered a door. Oinos lit a lamp next to an icon on the wall.

The icon looked like starlight. It showed angels praying at the left, and then the studded sapphiric canopy of the night sky behind a land with herbs shooting from the earth, and on the right an immense Man—if he was a Man—standing, his hand raised in benediction. All around the sapphire dome were some majestic figures, soaring aloft in two of their six wings. Art paused to drink it in.

"What are those symbols?"

"They are Greek letters. You are looking at an icon of the creation of the stars, but the text is not the text for that day; it is from another book, telling of the angels thunderously shouting for joy when the stars were created. So the stars are connected with the angels."

"Is this astrology?"

"No, because the stars and angels both point to God.

The influences in astrology point beyond matter to
something else, but they do not point far enough beyond
themselves. If you can use something to make a forecast
that way, it doesn't point far enough beyond itself."

"Why not?"

"One definition to distinguish religion from magic—one
used by anthropologists—is that religion is trying to come
into contact with the divine, and magic is trying to control
the divine. God cannot be controlled, and there is
something of control in trying to foretell a future that God
holds in mystery. A real God cannot be pried into by a skill.
Astrology departs from a science that can only see stars as
so much plasma, but it doesn't go far enough to lead people
to look into the stars and see a shadow of their Creator. To
be a sacred science, it is not enough to point to something
more than matter as secular science understands it; as the
term is used in our language, one can only be a *sacred*
science by pointing to God."

"Then what is a sacred science? Which branches of
learning as you break them up? Can they even be translated
into my language?"

"You seem to think that if astrology is not a sacred
science then sacred sciences must be something much more
hidden. Not so. Farming is a sacred science, as is hunting,
or inventing, or writing. When a monk makes incense, it is
not about how much incense he can make per unit of time;
his making incense is the active part of living
contemplatively, and his prayer shows itself in physical
labor. His act is more than material production; it is a
sacred science, or sacred art or sacred endeavor, and what
goes into and what comes out of the activity is prayer. Nor is
it simply a matter that he is praying while he acts; his
prayers matter for the incense. There are many lands from
your world's Desert Fathers to Mexico in your own day
where people have a sense that it matters what state people
cook in, and that cooking with love puts something into a
dish that no money can buy. Perhaps you will not look at me

askance when I say that not only monks in their monasteries exotically making incense for worship are performing a sacred science, but cooking, for people who may be low on the totem pole and who are not considered exotic, as much as for anyone else, can and should be a sacred science. Like the great work that will stay up with a sick child all night."

"Hmm..." Art said, and then finished his tankard. "Have you traveled much?"

"I have not reached one in five of the galaxies with inhabited worlds. I can introduce you to people who have some traveling experience, but I am not an experienced traveler. Still, I have met sites worth visiting. I have met, learned, worshiped. Traveling in this castle I have drunk the blood of gems. There are worlds where there is nothing to see, for all is music, and song does everything that words do for you. I have beheld a star as it formed, and I have been part of an invention that moves forward as a thousand races in their laboratories add their devices. I have read books, and what is more I have spoken with members of different worlds and races. There seems to be no shortage of wonders, and I have even been to your own world, with people who write fantasy that continues to astonish us—"

"My son-in-law is big into fantasy—he got me to see a Lord of the whatever-it-was movie—but I don't fancy them much myself."

"We know about Tolkein, but he is not considered a source of astonishing fantasy to us."

"Um..." Art took a long time to recall a name, and Oinos waited patiently. "Lewis?"

"If you're looking for names you would have heard of, Voltaire and Jung are two of the fantasy authors we consider essential. Tolkein and Lewis are merely imaginative. It is Voltaire and Jung who are truly fantasy authors. But there are innumerable others in your world."

Art said, "Um... what do you mean by 'fantasy author'?"

Oinos turned. "I'm sorry; there is a discrepancy between

how your language uses 'fantasy author' and ours. We have
two separate words that your 'fantasy' translates, and the
words stand for very different concepts. One refers to works
of imagination that are set in another world that is not
confused with reality. The other refers to a fundamental
confusion that can cost a terrible price. Our world does not
produce fiction; we do appreciate the fiction of other
worlds, but we do not draw a particularly strong line
between fiction where only the characters and events are
imagined, and fiction where the whole world is imagined.
But we do pay considerable attention to the second kind of
fantasy, and our study of fantasy authors is not a study of
imagination but a study of works that lead people into
unreality. 'Fantasy author' is one of the more important
terms in understanding your world and its history."

Art failed to conceal his reaction.

"Or perhaps I was being too blunt. But, unfashionable
as it may be, there is such a thing as evil in your world, and
the ways in which people live, including what they believe,
has something to do with it. Not everything, but
something."

Oinos waited for a time. Then, when Art remained
silent, he said, "Come with me. I have something to show
you." He opened a door on the other side of the room, and
went into the next room. The room was lit by diffuse
moonlight, and there was a ledge around the room and
water which Oinos stirred with his hand to light a
phosphorescent glow. When Art had stepped in, Oinos
stepped up, balancing on a steel cable, and stood silent for a
while. "Is there anything here that you can focus on?"

"What do you mean?"

"Step up on this cable and take my hand."

"What if I fall into the water?"

Art tried to balance, but it seemed even more difficult in
the dark. For a while, he tried to keep his balance with
Oinos's help, but he seemed barely up. He overcompensated
twice in opposite directions, began flying into the water,

and was stopped at last by Oinos's grip, strong as steel, on his arm.

"I can't do this," Art said.

"Very well." Oinos opened a door on the other side of the room, and slowly led him out. As they walked, Oinos started up a spiral staircase and sat down to rest after Art reached the top. Then Art looked up at the sky, and down to see what looked like a telescope.

"What is it?"

"A telescope, not too different from those of your world."

Oinos stood up, looked at it, and began some adjustments. Then he called Art over, and said, "Do you see that body?"

"What is it?"

"A small moon."

Oinos said, "I want you to look at it as closely as you can," and then pulled something on the telescope.

"It's moving out of sight."

"That's right; I just deactivated the tracking feature. You should be able to feel handles; you can move the telescope with them."

"Why do I need to move the telescope? Is the moon moving?"

"This planet is rotating: what the telescope sees will change as it rotates with the planet, and on a telescope you can see the rotation."

Art moved the handles and found that it seemed either not to move at all or else move a lot when he put pressure on it.

Art said, "This is a hard telescope to control."

Oinos said, "The telescope is worth controlling."

"Can you turn the tracking back on?"

Oinos merely repeated, "The telescope is worth controlling."

The celestial body had moved out of view. Art made several movements, barely passed over the moon, and then found it. He tried to see what he could, then give a relatively violent shove when the moon reached the edge of his field of view, and see if he could observe the body that way. After several tries, he began to get the object consistently in view... and found that he was seeing the same things about it, not being settled enough between jolts to really focus on what was there.

Art tried to make a smooth, slow movement with his body, and found that a much taller order than it sounded. His movement, which he could have sworn was gentle and smooth, produced what seemed like erratic movement, and it was only with greatest difficulty that he held the moon in view.

"Is this badly lubricated? Or do you have lubrication in this world?"

"We do, on some of our less precise machines. This telescope is massive, but it's not something that moves roughly when it is pushed smoothly; the joints move so smoothly that putting oil or other lubricants that are familiar to you would make them move much more roughly."

"Then why is it moving roughly every time I push it smoothly?"

"Maybe you aren't pushing it as smoothly as you think you are?"

Art pushed back his irritation, and then found the moon again. And found, to his dismay, that when the telescope jerked, he had moved the slightest amount unevenly.

Art pushed observation of the moon to the back of his mind. He wanted to move the telescope smoothly enough that he wouldn't have to keep finding the moon again. After a while, he found that this was less difficult than he thought, and tried for something harder: keeping the moon in the center of what he could see in the telescope.

He found, after a while, that he could keep the moon in the center if he tried, and for periods was able to manage something even harder: keeping the moon from moving, or perhaps just moving slowly. And then, after a time, he found himself concentrating through the telescope on taking in the beauty of the moon.

It was breathtaking, and Art later could never remember a time he had looked on something with quite that fascination.

Then Art realized he was exhausted, and began to sit down; Oinos pulled him to a bench.

After closing his eyes for a while, Art said, "This was a magnificent break from your teaching."

"A break from teaching? What would you mean?"

Art sat, opened his mouth, and then closed it. After a while, he said, "I was thinking about what you said about fantasy authors... do you think there is anything that can help?"

Oinos said, "Let me show you." He led Art into a long corridor with smooth walls and a round arch at top. A faint blue glow followed them, vanishing at the edges. Art said, "Do you think it will be long before our world has full artificial intelligence?"

Oinos said, "Hmm... Programming artificial intelligence on a computer is not *that* much more complex than getting a stone to lay an egg."

Art said, "But our scientists are making progress. Your advanced world has artificial intelligence, right?"

Oinos said, "Why on earth would we be able to do that? Why would that even be a goal?"

"You have computers, right?"

"Yes, indeed; the table that I used to call up a scientific calculator works on the same principle as your world's computers. I could almost say that inventing a new kind of computer is a rite of passage among serious inventors, or at least that's the closest term your world would have."

"And your computer science is pretty advanced, right? Much more advanced than ours?"

"We know things that the trajectory of computer science in your world will never reach because it is not pointed in the right direction." Oinos tapped the wall and arcs of pale blue light spun out.

"Then you should be well beyond the point of making artificial intelligence."

"Why on a million, million worlds should we ever be able to do that? Or even think that is something we *could* accomplish?"

"Well, if I can be obvious, the brain is a computer, and the mind is its software."

"Is it?"

"What else could the mind be?"

"What else could the mind be? What about an altar at which to worship? A workshop? A bridge between Heaven and earth, a meeting place where eternity meets time? A treasury in which to gather riches? A spark of divine fire? A line in a strong grid? A river, ever flowing, ever full? A tree reaching to Heaven while its roots grasp the earth? A mountain made immovable for the greatest storm? A home in which to live and a ship by which to sail? A constellation of stars? A temple that sanctifies the earth? A force to draw things in? A captain directing a starship or a voyager who can travel without? A diamond forged over aeons from of old? A perpetual motion machine that is simply impossible but functions anyway? A faithful manuscript by which an ancient book passes on? A showcase of holy icons? A mirror, clear or clouded? A wind which can never be pinned down? A haunting moment? A home with which to welcome others, and a mouth with which to kiss? A strand of a web? An acrobat balancing for his whole life long on a slender crystalline prism between two chasms? A protecting veil and a concealing mist? An eye to glimpse the uncreated Light as the world moves on its way? A rift yawning into the depths of the earth? A kairometer, both primeval and young? A—"

"All right, all right! I get the idea, and that's some pretty lovely poetry. (What's a kairometer?) These are all very beautiful metaphors for the mind, but I am interested in what the mind is literally."

"Then it might interest you to hear that your world's computer is also a metaphor for the mind. A good and poetic metaphor, perhaps, but a metaphor, and one that is better to balance with other complementary metaphors. It is the habit of some in your world to understand the human mind through the metaphor of the latest technology for you to be infatuated with. Today, the mind is a computer, or something like that. Before you had the computer, 'You're just wired that way' because the brain or the mind or whatever is a wired-up telephone exchange, the telephone exchange being your previous object of technological infatuation, before the computer. Admittedly, 'the mind is a computer' is an attractive metaphor. But there is some fundamental confusion in taking *that* metaphor literally and assuming that, since the mind is a computer, all you have to do is make some more progress with technology and research and you can give a computer an intelligent mind."

"I know that computers don't have emotions yet, but they seem to have rationality down cold."

"Do they?"

"Are you actually going to tell me that computers, with their math and logic, aren't rational?"

"Let me ask you a question. Would you say that the thing you can hold, a thing that you call a book, can make an argument?"

"Yes; I've seen some pretty good ones."

"Really? How do paper and ink think out their position?"

Art hesitated, and said, "Um, if you're going to nitpick..."

"I'm not nitpicking. A book is a tool of intelligent communication, and they are part of how people read author's stories, or explanation of how to do things, or poetry, or ideas. But the physical thing is not thereby intelligent. However much you think of a book as making an argument, the book is incapable of knowing what an argument is, and for that matter the paper and ink have no idea of whether they contain the world's best classic, or something mediocre, or incoherent accusations that world leaders are secretly planning to turn your world to dog drool, or randomly generated material that is absolute gibberish. The book may be meaningful to you, but the paper with ink on it is not the sort of thing that can understand what you recognize through the book.

"This might ordinarily be nitpicking, but it says something important about computers. One of the most difficult things for computer science instructors in your world to pound through people's heads is that a computer does not get the gist of what you are asking it to do and overlook minor mistakes, because the computer has no sense of what you are doing and no way to discern what were trying to get it to do from a mistake where you wrote in a bug by telling it to do something slightly different from what you meant. The computer has no sense that a programmer meant anything. A computer follows instructions, one after another, whether or not they make sense, and indeed without being able to wonder whether they make sense. To you, a program may be a tool that acts as an electronic shopping cart to let you order things through the web, but the web server no more understands that it is being used as a web server than a humor book understands that it is meant to make people laugh. Now most or all of the books you see are meant to say something —there's not much market for a paperback volume filled with random gibberish—but a computer can't understand that it is running a program written for a purpose any more than a book can understand that the ink on its pages is intended for people to read."

Art said, "You don't think artificial intelligence is making real progress? They seem to keep making new achievements."

Oinos said, "The rhetoric of 'We're making real breakthroughs now; we're on the verge of full artificial intelligence, and with what we're achieving, full artificial intelligence is just around the corner' is not new: people have been saying that full artificial intelligence is just around the corner since before you were born. But *breeding a better and better kind of apple tree is not progress towards growing oranges*. Computer science, and not just artificial intelligence, has gotten good at getting computers to function better as computers. But human intelligence is something else... and it is profoundly missing the point to only realize that the computer is missing a crucial ingredient of the most computer-like activity of human rational analysis. Even if asking a computer to recognize a program's purpose reflects a fundamental error—you're barking up the wrong telephone pole. Some people from your world say that when you have a hammer, everything begins to look like a nail. The most interesting thing about the mind is not that it can do something more complete when it pounds in computer-style nails. It's something else entirely."

"But what?"

"When things are going well, the 'computer' that performs calculating analysis is like your moon: a satellite, that reflects light from something greater. Its light is useful, but there is something more to be had. The sun, as it were, is that the mind is like an altar, or even something better. It takes long struggles and work, but you need to understand that the heart of the mind is at once practical and spiritual, and that its greatest fruit comes not in speech but in silence."

Art was silent for a long time.

Oinos stopped, tapped a wall once, and waited as an opening appeared in the black stone. Inside an alcove was a small piece of rough hewn obsidian; Oinos reached in, took it, and turned it to reveal another side, finely machined, with a series of concentric ridged grooves centered around a tiny niche. "You asked what a kairometer was, and this is a kairometer, although it would take you some time to understand exactly what it is."

"Is it one of the other types of computers in your world?"

"Yes. I would call it information technology, although not like the information technology you know. It is something people come back to, something by which people get something more than they had, but it does this not so much according to its current state as to our state in the moment we are using it. It does not change." Oinos placed the object in Art's hands.

Art slowly turned it. "Will our world have anything like this?"

Oinos took the kairometer back and returned it to its niche; when he withdrew his hand, the opening closed with a faint whine. "I will leave you to find that yourself."

Oinos began walking, and they soon reached the end of the corridor. Art followed Oinos through the doorway at the end and gasped.

Through the doorway was something that left Art trying to figure out whether or not it was a room. It was a massive place, lit by a crystalline blue light. As Art looked around, he began to make sense of his surroundings: there were some bright things, lower down, in an immense room with rounded arches and a dome at the top, made of pure glass. Starlight streamed in. Art stepped through the doorway and sunk down a couple of inches.

Oinos stooped for a moment, and then said, "Take off your shoes. They are not needed here." Art did so, and found that he was walking on a floor of velveteen softness. In the far heart of the room a thin plume of smoke arose. Art could not tell whether he smelled a fragrance, but he realized there was a piercing chant. Art asked, "What is the chant saying?"

Oinos did not answer.

What was the occasion? Art continued to look, to listen, and began trying to drink it in. It almost sounded as if they were preparing to receive a person of considerable importance. There was majesty in the air.

Oinos seemed to have slipped away.

Art turned and saw an icon behind him, hanging on the glass. There was something about it he couldn't describe. The icon was dark, and the colors were bright, almost luminous. A man lay dreaming at the bottom, and something reached up to a light hidden in the clouds—was it a ladder? Art told himself the artistic effect was impressive, but there was something that seemed amiss in that way of looking at it.

What bothered him about saying the icon had good artistic effect? Was the artistry bad? That didn't seem to be it. He looked at a couple of areas of artistic technique, but it was difficult to do so; such analysis felt like a foreign intrusion. He thought about his mood, but that seemed to be the wrong place to look, and almost the same kind of intrusion. There seemed to be something shining through the icon; looking at it was like other things he had done in this world, only moreso. He was looking through the icon and not around it, but... Art had some sense of what it was, but it was not something he could fit into words.

After being absorbed in the icon, Art looked around. There must have been hundreds of icons around, and lights, and people; he saw what seemed like a sparse number of people—of Oinos's kind—spread out through the vast space. There was a chant of some kind that changed from time to time, but seemed to somehow be part of the same flow. Things seemed to move very slowly—or move in a different time, as if clock time were turned on its side, or perhaps as if he had known clock time as it was turned on its side and now it was right side up—but Art never had the sense of nothing going on. There seemed to always be something more going on than he could grasp.

Art shifted about, having stood for what seemed like too long, sat down for a time, and stood up. The place seemed chaotic, in a way cluttered, yet when he looked at the "clutter," there was something shining through, clean as ice, majestic as starlight, resonant as silence, full of life as the power beneath the surface of a river, and ordered with an order that no rectangular grid could match. He did not understand any of the details of the brilliant dazzling darkness... but they spoke to him none the less.

After long hours of listening to the chant, Art realized with a start that the fingers of dawn had stolen all around him, and he saw stone and verdant forest about the glass walls until the sunlight began to blaze. He thought, he though he could understand the song even as its words remained beyond his reach, and he wished the light would grow stronger so he could see more. There was a crescendo all about him, and—

Oinos was before him. Perhaps for some time.

"I almost understand it," Art said. "I have started to taste this world."

Oinos bowed deeply. "It is time for you to leave."

The Spectacles

I got up, washed my face in the fountain, and put out the fire. The fountain was carved of yellow marble, set in the wall and adorned with bas-relief sculptures and dark moss. I moved through the labyrinth, not distracting myself with a lamp, not thinking about the organ, whose pipes ranged from 8' to 128' and could shake a cathedral to its foundation. Climbing iron rungs, I emerged from the recesses of a cluttered shed.

I was wearing a T-shirt advertising some random product, jeans which were worn at the cuffs, and fairly new tennis shoes. I would have liked to think I gave no hint of anything unusual: an ordinary man, with a messy house stocked with the usual array of mundane items. I blended in with the Illusion.

I drove over to Benjamin's house. As I walked in, I said, "Benjamin, I'm impressed. You've done a nice job of patching this place since the last explosion."

"Shut up, Morgan."

"By the way, my nephews are coming to visit in two weeks, Friday afternoon. Would you be willing to tinker in your laboratory when they come? Their favorite thing in the world is a good fireworks display."

"Which reminds me, there was one spice that I wanted to give you. It makes any food taste better, and the more you add, the better the food tastes. Pay no attention to the label on the bottle which says 'arsenic'. If you'll excuse me one moment..." He began to stand up, and I grabbed his shoulder and pulled him back down into the chair.

"How are you, Benjamin?"

"How are you, Morgan?"

I sat silent for a while. When Benjamin remained silent, I said, "I've been spending a lot of time in the library. The sense one gets when contemplating an artistic masterwork is concentrated in looking at what effect *The Mystical Theology* had on a thousand years of wonder."

He said, "You miss the Middle Ages, don't you?"

I said, "They're still around—a bit here, a piece there. On one hand, it's very romantic to hold something small in your hand and say that it is all that is left of a once great realm. On the other hand, it's *only* romantic: it is not the same thing as finding that glory all about you.

"The pain is all the worse when you not only come from a forgotten realm, but you must reckon with the Illusion. It's like there's a filter which turns everything grey. It's not exactly that there's a sinister hand that forces cooperation with the Illusion and tortures you if you don't; in some ways things would be simpler if there were. Of course you're asking for trouble if you show an anachronism in the way you dress, or if you're so gauche as to speak honestly out of the wisdom of another world and push one of the hot buttons of whatever today's hot issues are. But beyond that, you don't have to intentionally cooperate with the Illusion; you can 'non-conform freely' and the Illusion freely conforms itself to you. It's a terribly isolating feeling."

Benjamin stood up, walked over to a bookshelf, and pulled out an ivory tube. "I have something for you, Morgan. A pair of spectacles."

"Did you make these?"

"I'm not saying."

"Why are you giving me eyeglasses? My eyes are fine."

"Your eyes are weaker than you think." He waited a

moment, and then said, "And these spectacles have a virtue."

"What is their virtue? What is their power?"

"Please forgive me. As one who has struggled with the Illusion, you know well enough what it means to deeply want to convey something and know that you can't. Please believe me when I say that I would like to express the answer to your question, but I cannot."

I left, taking the glasses and both hoping that I was concealing my anger from Benjamin and knowing that I wasn't.

I arrived at home and disappeared into the labyrinth. A bright lamp, I hoped, would help me understand the spectacles' power. Had I been in a different frame of mind, I might have enjoyed it; I read an ancient and mostly complete Greek manuscript to *The Symbolic Theology* to see if it might reveal new insights. My eyes lingered for a moment over the words:

> That symbol, as most, has two layers. Yet a symbol could have an infinite number of layers and still be smaller than what is without layer at all.

I had a deep insight of some sort over these words, and the insight is forever lost because I cared only about one thing, finding out what magic power the spectacles held. I tried to read a cuneiform tablet; as usual, the language gave me an embarrassing amount of trouble, and there was something strange about what it said that completely lacked the allure of being exotic. Wishing I had a better command of languages, I moved about from one serpentine passageway to another, looking at places, even improvising on the organ, and enjoying none of it. Everything looked exactly as if I were looking through a children's toy. Had

Benjamin been watching too much *Dumbo* and given me a
magic feather?

After a long and fruitless search, I went up into my
house, put the spectacles in your pocket, and sat in my
chair, the lights off, fatigued in mind and body. I do not
recall know how long I stayed there. I only know that I
jumped when the doorbell rang.

It was Amber. She said, "The supermarket had a really
good sale on strawberries, and I thought you might like
some."

"Do you have a moment to to come in? I have Coke in
the fridge."

I had to stifle my urge to ask her opinion about the
spectacles' virtue. I did not know her to be more than meets
the eye (at least not in the sense that could be said of
Benjamin or me), but the Illusion was much weaker in her
than in most people, and she seemed to pick up on things
that I wished others would as well. We talked for a little
while; she described how she took her family to a pizza
restaurant and her son "walked up to a soda machine,
pushed one of the levers you're supposed to put your cup
against, jumped in startlement when soda fell on his hand,
and then began to lick the soda off."

"I've got to get home and get dinner on, but—ooh, you
have new glasses in your pocket. Put them on for a
moment."

I put my spectacles on, and she said something to me,
but I have no idea what she said. It's not because I was
drained: I was quite drained when she came, but her charm
had left me interested in life again. The reason I have no
idea what she said to me is that I was stunned at what I saw
when I looked at her through the spectacles.

I saw beauty such as I had not begun to guess at. She
was clad in a shimmering robe of scintillating colors. In one
hand, she was holding a kaliedoscope, which had not semi-
opaque colored chips but tiny glass spheres and prisms
inside. The other hand embraced a child on her lap, with

love so real it could be seen.

After she left, I took the spectacles off, put them in their case, and after miscellaneous nightly activities, went to bed and dreamed dreams both brilliant and intense.

When I woke up, I tried to think about why I had not recognized Amber's identity before. I closed my eyes and filtered through memories; Amber had given signals of something interesting that I had not picked up on—and she had picked up on things I had given. I thought of myself as one above the Illusion—and here I had accepted the Illusion's picture of her. Might there be others who were more than meets the eye?

I came to carry the spectacles with me, and look around for a sign of something out of the ordinary. Several days later, I met a tall man with cornrowed greying hair. When I asked him what he studied in college, he first commented on the arbitrariness of divisions between disciplines, before explaining that his discipline of record was philosophy. His thought was a textbook example of postmodernism, but when I put my spectacles on, I saw many translucent layers: each layer, like a ring of an oak, carried a remnant of a bygone age. Then I listened, and his words sounded no less postmodern, but echoes of the Middle Ages were everywhere.

I began to find these people more and more frequently, and require less and less blatant cues.

I sat in the living room, waiting with cans of Coca-Cola. I enjoy travelling in my nephews' realms; at a prior visit, Nathan discovered a whole realm behind my staircase, and it is my loss that I can only get in when I am with him. Brandon and Nathan had come for the fair that weekend, and I told them I had something neat-looking to show them before I took them to the fair.

I didn't realize my mistake until they insisted that I wear the spectacles at the fair.

I didn't mind the charge of public drunkenness *that* much. It was humiliating, perhaps, but I think at least *some* humiliations are necessary in life. And I didn't mind too much that my nephews' visit was a bummer for them. Perhaps that was unfortunate, but that has long been smoothed over. There were, however, two things that were *not* of small consequence to me.

The first thing that left me staggered was something in addition to the majesty I saw. I saw a knight, clad in armor forged of solid light, and I saw deep scars he earned warring against dragons. I saw a fair lady who looked beautiful at the skin when seen without the spectacles, and beautiful in layer after layer below the skin when seen with them. The something else I saw in addition to that majesty was that this beauty was something that was not just in a few people, or even many. It was in every single person without exception. That drunken beggar everyone avoided, the one with a stench like a brewery next to a horse stable—I saw his deep and loyal friendships. I saw his generosity with other beggars—please believe me that if you were another beggar, what's his was yours. I saw the quests he made in his youth. I saw his dreams. I saw his story. Beyond all that, I saw something deeper than any of these, a glory underneath and beneath these things. This glory, however disfigured by his bondage to alcohol, filled me with wonder.

The reason the police kept me in the drunk tank for so long was that I was stunned and reeling. I had always known that I was more than what the Illusion says a person is, and struggled to convey my something more to other people... but I never looked to see how other people could be more than the grey mask the Illusion put on their faces. When I was in the drunk tank, I looked at the other men in wonder and asked myself what magic lay in them, what my spectacles would tell me. The old man with an anchor tattooed to his arm: was he a sailor? Where had he sailed on the seven seas? Had he met mermaids? I almost asked him if he'd found Atlantis, when I decided I didn't want to prolong the time the police officer thought I was drunk.

This brings me to the second disturbing find, which was that my spectacles were not with me. I assumed this was because the police had locked them away, but even after I was released, determined inquiry found no one who had seen them. They looked interesting, oddly shaped lenses with thick gold frames; had a thief taken them when I was stunned and before the police picked me up?

The next day I began preparing for a quest.

It filled me with excitement to begin searching the black market, both because I hoped to find the spectacles, and because I knew I would experience these people in a completely new light.

I had dealings with the black market before, but it had always been unpleasant: not (let me be clear) because I did not know how to defend myself, or was in too much danger of getting suckered into something dangerous, but because I approached its people concealing the emotions I'd feel touching some kind of fetid slime. Now... I still saw that, but I tried to look and see what I would see if I were wearing my spectacles.

I didn't find anything that seemed significant. The next leg of my journey entailed a change of venue: I dressed nicely and mingled with the world of jewellers and antique dealers. Nada.

I began to search high and low; I brainstormed about what exotic places it might be, and I found interesting people along the way. The laborers whom I hired to help me search the city dump almost made me forget that I was searching for something, and over time I chose to look for my spectacles in places that would bring me into contact with people I wanted to meet...

Some years later, I was returning from one of my voyages and realized it had been long (*too* long) since I had spoken with Benjamin. I came and visited him, and told him about the people I'd met. After I had talked for an hour, he put his hand on my mouth and said, "Can I get a word in edgewise?"

I said, "Mmmph mph mmmph mmph."

He took his hand off my mouth, and I said, "That depends on whether you're rude enough to put your hand over my mouth in mid-sentence."

"That depends on whether you're rude enough to talk for an hour without letting your host get a word in edgewise."

I stuck my tongue out at him.

He stuck his tongue out at me.

Benjamin opened a box on his desk, opened the ivory case inside the box, and pulled out my spectacles. "I believe these might interest you." He handed them to me.

I sat in silence. The clock's ticking seemed to grow louder, until it chimed and we both jumped. Then I looked at him and said, "What in Heaven's name would I need them for?"

Milton Keynes UK
Ingram Content Group UK Ltd.
UKHW020316070624
443692UK00003B/76